SET ME FREE

Pack Law 1

Becca Van

MENAGE EVERLASTING

Siren Publishing, Inc.
www.SirenPublishing.com

A SIREN PUBLISHING BOOK
IMPRINT: Ménage Everlasting

SET ME FREE
Copyright © 2012 by Becca Van

ISBN: 978-1-62241-038-5

First Printing: June 2012

Cover design by Les Byerley
All art and logo copyright © 2012 by Siren Publishing, Inc.

Printed in the U.S.A.

PUBLISHER
Siren Publishing, Inc.
www.SirenPublishing.com

DEDICATION

I would like to dedicate this book to all the people who contact me through Facebook and for letting me know what you think of my stories. Thank you for your continued support. This one is for you.

SET ME FREE

Pack Law 1

BECCA VAN

Chapter One

"Don't eat me! Good doggy. Please leave. I promise, I don't taste very nice," Michelle Barclay told the wolflike dog standing before her, its tongue lolling out the side of its mouth as she pressed herself up against her small compact car in the secluded parking lot of the library.

Michelle Barclay had only been in Aztec, New Mexico, for three weeks. She had decided to move from her home state of Nebraska when she had received a letter from lawyers Holt and Holt six months ago declaring her the owner of a small rural property in the town. She was now working as a librarian. For four months she had pondered over whether or not to sell the property and buy her own place in her hometown of Mullen, but the thought of being in a small rural town and not having to pay rent anymore was too good to ignore. So she had given notice and moved to the small cottage five minutes outside of the town of Aztec. She was a twenty-six-year-old librarian and had never been on a date. At first she was too busy with her studies, and then she had just never found anyone who engaged her brain as well as her body. She knew she was seen as an uptight schoolmarm, as she dressed so conservatively, but she just didn't give a damn about what anyone else thought. She wasn't about to lower her standards for anyone. No matter who they were.

Michelle felt behind her for the keyhole with the tip of her finger and thanked God she'd had the foresight to have her car keys in her hand. She jiggled the key, trying to get the metal to slide into the lock, but since she kept her eyes on the now-sitting wolf-dog before her, she was having a hell of a time trying to fit the key in the lock. Every time she tried to move, the animal before her would begin to growl, its hackles rising on the back of its neck. The muscles in its huge body would ripple as it tensed up, looking like it was ready to pounce on her.

Michelle couldn't work out if the animal in front of her was a wolf, a dog, or a combination of both. The animal was huge. When it was standing up on all four paws, the top of its head was level with her chest. She kept looking around to see if its owner was nearby, but the brightly lit parking lot and street looked to be totally deserted. She looked into the dog's gray eyes and breathed in deeply, held the breath, and released it slowly.

"Look, I don't know what you want, but I need to get home. I'm going to turn around, open my car door, get in, and leave, all right?" Michelle said, then slowly turned her body sideways, making sure she could still see the animal as she finally got her key into the lock. The sound of the snick on her older-style car seemed really loud in the still night air.

Michelle cringed as the wolf-dog slowly walked toward her, its steely-gray eyes holding hers, until she could feel its hot breath on her arm. She whimpered with fear and nearly jumped out of her skin as the animal's mouth wrapped around her left wrist. She waited for the excruciating pain she knew would follow as the animal clamped down with its powerful jaw, but the pain never came. She opened eyes she hadn't realized she'd closed and stared at the dog. The sound of footsteps echoing behind her had her sagging against her car with relief.

"Are you all right, miss…?" A deep, gravelly voice came from behind her.

"I will be if you can get this–this dog to let me get into my car," Michelle said quietly so as not to alarm the dog, but loud enough for whoever was near to hear. She heard the man behind her move around the back of her car and then heard him snap out a command to the animal still gently holding her wrist.

"Mikhail, let her go. Now!" The man growled.

To Michelle's surprise the animal released her and licked the sensitive skin on her inner wrist, making a hysterical giggle bubble up from her chest as its warm, wet tongue tickled her skin.

"What are you doing out here alone on a Friday night, ma'am?" the man asked as he moved forward into her vision.

Michelle's breath caught in her throat at the first sight of the owner of the deep, sinful, gravelly voice. He was tall, so much taller than her own height of five foot four inches. He stood around six foot one and had sandy-brown hair, a lean, rangy muscularity, and deep-blue eyes. He had a high forehead, a beaklike nose, sharp cheekbones, full red lips, and a hard, rugged jaw. His stance was confident and aggressive. His arms were crossed over a muscular chest, his hips thrust slightly forward, his legs shoulder width apart, but his eyes were what captured her the most. His eyes seemed to glow as he stood staring at her. She moved her eyes back to his mouth and was just in time to see his nostrils flare above those full, sexy lips as he inhaled. She could have sworn she heard him growl before he shifted on his feet and moved in closer toward her.

"I haven't seen you around here before. Are you new to town or just passing through?" he asked as he stopped inches away from her.

"I moved here three weeks ago. I work at the library and was just leaving for the night," Michelle replied, her eyes sliding from his to the dog now sitting quietly next to him. She felt hemmed in and didn't like to feel so crowded. Her breathing escalated and she tried to push herself further into the protection of her old car.

"Hm, you must be Michelle Barclay. I'm Jonah Friess, a member of the library board. Pleased to meet you, Michelle," Jonah said as he held his hand out in greeting.

"Mr. Friess," Michelle replied, slipping her hand into his. She couldn't quite contain a gasp of shock as she felt a spark of electricity race up her arm, over her chest, and down to her pussy. She'd never felt anything like it before. Her vagina clenched, and she felt moisture drip down to wet her panties. She tried to snatch her hand away, but Jonah wouldn't let her. He tightened his grip, but he didn't hurt her.

Michelle felt her own nostrils flare as he took another step in closer to her body. The scent of musk, soap, and clean male assailed her olfactory sense. She tried to tug her hand away while keeping her breathing shallow, afraid her hard nipples and aching breasts would rub against his chest if she took a deeper breath. She held very still as Jonah leaned in close to her, bent his head down to her neck, and inhaled.

"You smell good. What perfume are you wearing?" Jonah asked.

Michelle cleared her throat, twice, before she could speak. The heat and nearness of his body was making her crazy. "I'm not. I don't wear any perfume. It must be the soap I used this morning that you can smell."

"Mmm," Jonah hummed. "You smell good enough to eat."

"P–Pardon?"

"I said, you smell good enough to eat," Jonah breathed against her ear.

"Mr. Friess, would you please move away? You're crowding me," Michelle stated indignantly. She felt a flutter against the top of her ear and wondered if the man had just licked her. *No, he couldn't have. My imagination is running rife tonight.*

"Is that your dog, Mr. Friess?" Michelle asked, looking to the animal again.

"I guess you could say that. My name is Jonah, darlin'. You calling me 'mister' makes me feel old."

"Um, well. Okay then, Jo–Jonah."

Michelle let out a sigh of relief as Jonah released her hand and stepped back. Now she could breathe. She moved away from her car door, grasped the handle, and opened it. She was about to slide into the seat, but the sound of Jonah's voice stopped her.

"Have you had dinner yet, Michelle?"

"Uh, no," Michelle replied, turning back to face Jonah. "I'm about to head home and prepare a light dinner."

"I haven't eaten yet either," Jonah said then looked at her expectantly.

Michelle knew Jonah was waiting for an invitation to dinner. As much as good manners were in ground in to her personality, Michelle found herself hesitating. The way the man was looking at her made her feel like prey to his predator. For some reason he turned her on, and she just wasn't comfortable with that unfamiliar sensation. It wasn't that she was afraid of him, it was the fact she was scared of her body's response.

"I'll leave you so you can go home and enjoy your meal then. Thanks for the help with your dog. He looks like a wolf, you know."

"That's because he is a wolf, darlin'. You don't have to worry about him hurting you. That couldn't be further from the truth."

"Well, if you say so. It was nice meeting you, Mr....Jonah."

"You have no idea, darlin'," Jonah replied cryptically.

Michelle gave Jonah a look with raised eyebrows, shook her head, and slid into the driver's seat of her car and left the parking lot. Glancing in the mirror, she noticed Jonah and his wolf watched her until she was out of sight. There was just something strange about that man. She couldn't put her finger on what it was that puzzled her, but even though the man turned her body inside out with unfamiliar desire, there was more to him than what was on the surface.

Michelle had heard about him and his two brothers since they were on the library board, but this was the first time she'd met one of the Friess men. She wracked her brain trying to remember what his brothers' names were as she drove along the dark outskirts of Aztec. Then it hit her. Their names were Jonah, Mikhail, and Brock Friess. How strange to name one's wolf after his brother. Surely the man could have come up with a better name. She wondered if his brother was insulted or flattered, then gave a mental shrug of indifference. Who cared what the man called his wolf? Why he wanted a wolf instead of a dog for a pet was beyond her comprehension.

Michelle sighed with relief as she pulled her 1984 model small car into her driveway. Once she got inside and closed the door behind her, she released her hair from the perpetual tight bun she kept it in and shook her long brown tresses free. She undid the top three buttons on her high-necked blouse as she kicked off her shoes and headed to her bedroom. She liked to keep her appearance professional when she worked at the library, but once she was home the façade came off. She removed her blouse and ankle-length skirt, unclipped her stockings from her garter belt, and rolled them down her legs. She took off the garter belt to be left standing in a red lace G-string and matching demi bra. She pulled her favorite jeans and large college T-shirt from her closet and drawer, then pulled them on. Once comfortable, she padded to her kitchen in bare feet and set about getting some dinner, but while she cooked, she couldn't get the memory of Jonah and his wolf-dog out of her mind.

Chapter Two

"Yes, she is our mate," Jonah replied verbally. "Go and change forms, get dressed, and meet me at Aztec's and bring Brock with you. We have some plans to map out."

Jonah and Mikhail watched as the woman of their dreams drove away. Jonah was about to enter the Aztec Club after a long workweek to grab a beer and unwind. He was just about to step through the doors to the club he and his brothers owned when Mikhail had called out to him telepathically. He felt his brother's excitement and arousal through their link and had turned toward the library parking lot at the end of the street. He was surprised to find his brother had cornered a woman up against her car in the library lot, but knew he must have had a damn good reason. Mikhail had never done anything like that before. As he'd moved closer, Jonah had caught a whiff of the woman's scent which had called out to his wolf. He knew in that instant the woman could possibly be the mate he and his two brothers had waited for. He had to make sure, so he had moved in close to her and sniffed her neck. He'd gone rock hard in an instant. The blood had drained from his brain straight down to his crotch, filling his cock so full, he ached. He'd had to push his beast back down as he could feel his wolf ramming at him to claim his mate. He'd been able to resist, *just*.

"*Mate,*" Mikhail growled into Jonah's mind.

Jonah watched as Mikhail took off, a dark blur of speed as he disappeared into the trees off to the side of the library building. He turned around and headed back down Main Street, his destination their very own Aztec Club.

* * * *

Jonah was sitting at their usual table when he scented the arrival of his brothers. He picked up his beer and took a sip then gestured for his brothers to sit when they arrived at their table. As firstborn and the most Alpha out of his brothers, his word was pack law. Even though his brothers were also Alphas, when Jonah laid down the law no one questioned him, not even his brothers. Of course he was always open to advice from any of his werewolves and often discussed pack and business issues with his brothers, but if he put his foot down, no one dared argue.

Jonah had been main Alpha of the pack since he was twenty years old. His father had handed over the reins to him when he and his mother had decided they wanted to take the time to travel. Jonah had been prepared to be Alpha of the pack along with his brothers since the day of their birth, but they had all known he was the most senior leader of the Friess pack as he was the eldest.

His cousins, Chris, Blayk, and James Friess, were his Betas, second to the Alphas, as were Jake, Devon, and Greg Domain, his cousins on his mother's side. The rest of the pack members were labeled as Omegas.

Jonah leaned back in his chair as he studied his brothers' excited expressions. He was feeling as excited and horny at just having met their mate, but he also knew they had a lot of work and planning to do. Their little mate seemed to be very shy and innocent, and the last thing he wanted was to scare her away.

"What does she look like?" Brock asked as he shifted in his seat.

"Like an uptight schoolmarm," Mikhail replied with a grin. "She's small and had her brown hair up in a tight bun, and her clothes were so long and shapeless I couldn't see her figure very well. She had her shirt buttoned up to the collar and her skirt was so long I couldn't even see her ankles. But her eyes, man, her eyes were such a light green they seemed to see into your soul. Boy, did she smell good. I got in a good whiff and could smell her creaming as she stood there staring at me and Jonah. Her heartbeat elevated and so did her breathing. She's just a little bit of a thing, my head came up to her chest when standing on all fours."

"If she's so shy and timid, how are we going to seduce her into our bed?" Brock asked.

"That's what we need to work out," Jonah replied. "How we are going to woo our mate?"

"I vote we just take her," Brock said with a lascivious waggle of his brows.

"Don't be stupid, Brock. You know that would never work. She'd run so far, so fast, you wouldn't see her backside disappear," Mikhail said with an impatient growl. "I think we should leave it up to Jonah to get her out to our place. She was panting so hard around him I thought she was gonna climax where she stood."

"Okay, I'll concede to that, but how are we going to get her into bed with all of us? Do you think she'll accept a ménage relationship?" Brock asked uncertainly.

"How the hell should we know?" Mikhail growled. "We should start off by inviting her for dinner."

"Yes, I think that could work. I know our mate is working tomorrow morning. I'll meet her when she gets off work at noon and invite her out to the den. You two are to be on your best behavior. I don't want you scaring her away by crowding her too much. She doesn't like to be hemmed in," Jonah stated.

"Fuck it, Jonah. How the hell are we going to get her to accept all three of us as her mates if she doesn't like being crowded?" Brock asked.

"One step at a time, brother, one step at a time," Jonah replied.

Jonah and his brothers spent the next few hours going over scenarios of how to woo their mate. They were interrupted frequently as pack members greeted and congratulated their Alphas at finally finding their mate. Mikhail had sent out a telepathic statement to the male pack members, informing them when he had gone home to change clothes. The solicitations had been coming thick and fast ever since.

Jonah scented Kirsten as soon as she walked in the door to the club. He groaned with resignation because he knew she was going to be trouble. She was an Omega, low down in the pack, and he and his brothers had been sharing her for sexual relief. He had made sure she knew the score, that he and his brothers were only using her for sex and as recently as last night. He was not looking forward to the coming confrontation. The din of chatter ceased as Kirsten moved through the tables and stopped when she arrived where they were sitting.

Jonah could tell she knew something was going on because all was quiet and she was looking around her curiously. She turned back to Jonah and his brothers, asking her question with the rise of an eyebrow.

"Alphas," Kirsten greeted. "What's going on?"

"Kirsten, take a seat," Jonah commanded and waited until she'd obeyed his order.

Jonah swept the crowd with a hard stare and was relieved when everyone began to talk amongst themselves once more. He waited until Kirsten had taken a sip of her chardonnay before he began to let her down easy.

"Kirsten, we have enjoyed you sharing your body with us, but I'm afraid we won't be having sex with you anymore," Jonah said quietly.

Jonah watched as the glass in Kirsten's hand wobbled and went the rest of the way to her lips as she took a sip.

"Why not? I thought you liked having sex with me?" Kirsten asked, no inflection in her voice.

"We do…did," Jonah corrected and sighed. He was going to have to be honest with her so he wouldn't hurt her feelings. Even though she sounded calm, he could see the hurt and turmoil in her eyes. "We've met our mate."

Jonah knew he'd hurt her with his words, and as much as that knowledge pained him, he and his brothers had been up-front with her from the start. There was nothing he could do about the way she felt. He watched as Kirsten placed her glass back on the table and rose to her feet. She bowed to him, not looking him in the eye, and spoke.

"Congratulations, Alphas. I think I'll have an early night."

Jonah and his brothers watched until she exited the club's door. Brock turned to Jonah, a scowl on his face.

"That went well," he said facetiously. "She's heartbroken, Jonah. Couldn't you have been easier on her?"

"What would you have me tell her, Brock? 'Thanks for the sex but we don't want you anymore?' She knew from the start it was only about the sex. I couldn't lie to her. Everyone already knows we've found our mate. She would have heard about it eventually and even though she may have feelings for us, she is not in love with us. Only a true mate can ever capture a *were's* heart. We all knew, including Kirsten, there was a possibility of us meeting our mate. We can't ignore the call to our hearts and bodies just to keep Kirsten happy for the short term," Jonah bit out.

"You couldn't have done anything different, Jonah," Mikhail advised. "She was going to get hurt no matter what you said. Let's get out of here. The sooner we go to sleep, the sooner our mate will be in our home."

"Good idea, brother, let's go," Jonah reiterated as he rose to his feet. He led the way out of the club, his brothers following close behind.

Chapter Three

Michelle had been at the library for an hour, steadily working through the stack of books needing to be put back on shelves. She was in the mythology section when she heard the bell over the door tinkle, notifying her of a library patron.

"I'll be with you in a minute," Michelle called as she placed the last two books in their proper alphabetical order. Once done, she made her way back to the counter, placing a welcoming smile on her face as she saw the blonde woman standing waiting for her. She walked around the end of the counter, feeling like a complete dowd as she eyed the sophisticated woman glaring at her.

"Can I help you?" Michelle asked politely as she took in the defensive stance of the tall blonde woman.

"Not really, I just had to come see the competition for myself," the woman spat. "I have no idea what they see in you. You're nothing but a mouse."

"Um, okay, I'm sorry but I have no idea what you're talking about," Michelle replied, turning the smile on her face to a frown.

"Just remember, they were mine until last night. You don't have what it takes to keep them. I'll be waiting in the wings, because they will come back to me, eventually. You're new, so you're a novelty for them. You don't have what it takes to keep them," the woman said, giving Michelle a disparaging look as her eyes slid from the top of her head down to her waist and back up again.

"I still don't know what you're talking about, miss... Who are they?"

"Don't worry, you'll find out soon enough," the woman said then leaned in closer. "They are mine and will be again. Don't forget, bye."

Michelle watched as the woman stormed out of the library. She wondered if she was a fruit loop, a sandwich short of a picnic. She was certainly out of her mind. She wasn't seeing one male, let alone "them," more than one man, whoever "them" was. She shook her head, sighed, and got back to work. She still had a lot of books to put away as well as paperwork to get through, and she was only working a half day since it was Saturday. There were never enough hours in the day.

Michelle had worked the morning away. She glanced up at the clock. She was getting hungry, and she still had half an hour before closing. Her head was beginning to ache, and her muscles were taut with tension and had been since her visitor this morning. She wanted nothing more than to pull her hair out from the tight bun she had it in, pull on her favorite jeans, grab a glass of wine, and curl up with one of her secret pleasures and while the afternoon away. Michelle always felt a little guilty whenever she pulled one of her erotic novels out and read it. She kept them hidden in the bottom of her closet away from prying eyes, not that she had any visitors, but she would be mortified if anyone ever discovered her wicked secret. She lowered her head and began to concentrate on her work once more.

Michelle had been so engrossed in what she was doing she didn't hear the bell on the door tinkle. She only became aware someone was standing before her as they cleared their throat to get her attention. She was so startled she jumped and nearly fell off her seat. She gripped the edge of the counter with her fingers, her head snapping up, and drowned. The sight of those familiar glowing blue eyes had her shifting on her stool as he stood leaning against the counter staring at her.

"I'm sorry. I didn't mean to scare you. I thought you'd heard me come in."

"No. I was so engrossed in my work I didn't hear the bell. How are you, Jonah?"

"I'm fine. And you?"

"Very well, thank you. Can I help you with anything?"

"As a matter of fact, you can. You can do me the honor of having lunch with me today," Jonah stated.

"Um, I don't think…" Michelle began only to be interrupted.

"Good, don't think. I'll wait for you to lock up," Jonah said as he looked around the room. "Since there is no one here and you only have fifteen minutes till the end of your shift, why don't you finish up now?"

"Oh, but that wouldn't be fair to whoever pays my wages. It would feel like I was stealing," Michelle said and didn't realize she'd lowered her voice to a whisper.

"No, it wouldn't. Since I'm the one who pays your wage and I'm here telling you to leave, you're not doing anything wrong. Come on, Michelle. Surely you're hungry?" Jonah asked persuasively.

"Um, well, yes, but I don't think it's a good idea…"

"I thought I told you not to think. What harm can it do to have a meal with your boss?" Jonah persuaded.

"Well, I suppose…" Michelle began, but the arrogant bastard cut her off again.

"Good. Why don't you shut down the computer and grab your things. I'll make sure everything else is turned off and locked up," Jonah commanded as he straightened, walked over to the light switches, and shut them off.

By the time Michelle was ready, Jonah was waiting for her at the door. He held the door open for her, set the alarm, and followed her out. Michelle let go of the library-door keys as if they burned her hand when Jonah reached to take them from her. The tingles erupting up and down the length of her spine gathered in her crotch, making her clit ache and pussy clench. She felt cream seep onto her panties, making them damp. *What is it about this man that has me so hot so fast?*

When Jonah handed her the keys back, she clutched them tightly in her hand, turned toward her car, and began to walk, and Jonah fell into step at her side. She had her car keys at the ready and slid the key into the lock only to hesitate when Jonah walked up close behind her. She could feel the body heat emanating from him but didn't turn around.

"Why don't we go in my car? I'll drive you back to yours later."

Michelle turned her head just in time to see Jonah lean down and inhale. She held very still and wondered what the hell he was doing and why he seemed to have an obsession for smelling her. She sighed out with relief as he stood up straight and took a couple of steps back. She turned to the side, her hand still on her keys.

"I'd rather drive my own car, Jonah. I like to be independent. I'll follow you if you'll lead the way," Michelle said, then relaxed as Jonah shrugged and walked to his truck. He had the engine running and was waiting on her by the time she was settled into her car and buckled in. She looked over and gave him a nod, letting him know she was ready.

Michelle took in the countryside once they had left the small town of Aztec behind. She'd never been this way before and took great delight in taking in the wide-open fields full of wildflowers and the native trees. She knew the spring flowers would soon wither and die as summer came to bear. The heat always killed off any blossoms quickly, and there never was enough rainfall in this part of the country to keep them hydrated. She was becoming anxious the farther away from Aztec they travelled and wondered just where the hell Jonah was leading her. She'd forgotten to ask where he was taking her for lunch, thinking it would be somewhere in Aztec. She was just about to stop her car and turn around when Jonah slowed his truck and turned into a driveway. She followed behind, taking in the large automatic gates and high fences surrounding the property. They travelled for another five hundred yards, and then she was gasping in awe.

The huge mansion with white columns on either side of the entry reminded her of the old movie with Scarlett O'Hara, *Gone with the Wind*. The house was three stories high and as wide as she'd ever seen. The man was obviously loaded. She followed his truck around the side of the house and pulled up behind him as he parked in a large carport. She turned off the engine and sat staring around her. The property had to be at least a couple of acres, and that was a guess because she couldn't see where the fence line ended.

Michelle opened her car door, got out, and tried not to flinch when Jonah helped her with a hand at her elbow. The man seemed to love touching her, and she wasn't used to being touched at all. She'd been abandoned as a baby and had lived in a convent and foster care. She'd never been hugged or touched as much in her life as she had since meeting Jonah Friess. She liked it, a lot, but was worried she would get used to it. The last thing she wanted to do was make a fool out of herself by reading more into his courteous actions and throwing herself at him like she wanted to. Just because a man had good manners and touched her while helping guide her or make sure she was steady on her feet, didn't mean he was attracted to her. But then if she had read his body language right, he didn't exactly find her abhorrent.

"Relax, Michelle. You have nothing to be afraid of. No one here would ever harm you," Jonah said as he slid his hand down her arm and clasped her hand in his. "Come on and we'll get some lunch. I employ a wonderful housekeeper, and she makes the best food. Are you hungry?"

Michelle's stomach took the opportune moment to growl loud enough for her to hear. She felt her face go red, but looked up at Jonah anyway. "It would seem so," she said with a smile and walked alongside Jonah as he led her to a door off the carport.

The smells which assailed her nostrils made her saliva glands work overtime and her stomach grumble even louder in anticipation. She let Jonah lead her into a hallway, then turned right and found herself the center of attention. Jonah had led her into a huge kitchen dining room. There were two women working in the kitchen, and the dining table was surrounded by men and a few women. She lowered her eyes and stared at her feet as all eyes turned toward her and Jonah.

"Michelle, I like you to meet my housekeeper, Angela, and her daughter, Cindy. Angie has worked in the house since I was a baby. She takes good care of everyone here, so if you ever need anything just ask Angela."

"Welcome, Michelle," Angela said.

"Thank you, it's nice to meet you, and you, too, Cindy," Michelle greeted both women.

"Come and sit down and I'll introduce you to everyone else," Jonah said and tugged on her hand gently, pulling her along with him.

Michelle followed Jonah to the other side of the long timber dining table. The room was nearly as big as her whole house, and the table was nearly as large. Jonah stopped at the end of the table where two empty chairs were waiting. Instead of sitting down, he waited until all eyes were on them and drew her in close to his side, wrapping his arm around her shoulders.

"Everyone, this is Michelle Barclay, she'll be joining us for lunch today. Michelle, I'll start on this side of the table and tell you everyone's names as we go around, but don't worry if you don't remember them all. Just ask if you forget people's names. We understand it takes time and can be overwhelming to meet such a large group of people," Jonah said. "This is my brother Mikhail, and next to him are our cousins Chris, Blayk, and James Friess. And more of our cousins on our mother's side of the family are Jake, Greg, and Devon Domain, who are seated from James down."

Michelle was lost after that. She tried to pick out features on people's faces to remember them, but there were just too many of them. She didn't realize she'd tuned out until she heard Jonah introducing another brother, Brock, who was seated to the left of where she stood. She gave him a polite smile, and then her smile widened as Brock burst out laughing. She had no idea what was so funny, but she could feel the tension draining from her at such a full-bodied belly laugh and the twinkle of mischief in Brock's eyes.

"Don't worry about remembering the names, baby. You'll have us all down pat before you know it," Brock said as he rose from his chair.

Michelle had to crick her neck to keep her eyes on his. The man was a veritable giant. He had to be at least a foot taller than she was, and boy, was he packed full of muscle. His shoulders were so wide he blocked out the light as he stood before her. His shoulders and pectoral muscles moved under the tight black T-shirt he wore. His abs rippled and tapered down into slim hips, strong, muscular thighs, and the longest legs she'd ever seen. She could feel her face heating as her libido once again decided to take control over her mind.

The sound of another male voice calling her name made her turn toward Mikhail. She felt a shiver race up her spine as she looked into Mikhail's silver-gray eyes and felt her pussy leak onto her panties. *God, what is wrong with me? It's bad enough lusting after one man, but three? Get a grip, Michelle.*

"Are you okay, honey? You look a little flushed," Mikhail asked, leaning toward her over the corner of the table.

"Yes, I'm fine. Just a little…overwhelmed," Michelle answered with a smile.

"Have a seat, baby," Brock said from behind her, pulled her chair back, and saw her seated, then took his own seat beside her. Jonah sat on her other side, and then Angela and her daughter began to bring platters laden with food to the table.

Michelle watched in awe as the men loaded their plates high with food and wondered where they put it all. Sure, they were all big, brawny, handsome men, but not one of them had an ounce of fat on their toned bodies. How the hell they could pack away so much food was beyond her.

Michelle saw Jonah whisk her plate up, and he began to fill it with food. He piled it with steak, salad, and vegetables. He'd given her enough food to feed her all week long. He placed the now-loaded plate before her, and she lowered her eyes and stared at it. There was no way she'd be able to eat all that.

"Eat up, darlin'," Jonah said as he began to eat.

Michelle ate some of the salad and a quarter of the large steak. She'd been thankful to find the housekeeper liked to cook her meat medium rare, just the way she liked it. She'd eaten way more than she usually did for lunch and sat back with a satisfied sigh after placing her utensils on her plate.

"You can't possibly have had enough, baby," Brock whispered, leaning toward her.

"I assure you I have. I usually only have a sandwich for lunch."

"Do you mind if I finish what you've left?" Brock asked, giving her a smirk, the sexy bastard.

"Sure, have at it," Michelle replied, pushing her plate toward him.

Chapter Four

A sound from across the room caught Michelle's attention. She raised her head to see the blonde woman who had visited her at the library that very morning. The beautiful woman was decked out in designer-label clothes, her makeup applied to perfection. It made Michelle feel like something the cat had dragged in from the yard in her dowdy schoolmarm clothes. But ever since she'd finished her degree in Mullen and been harassed by the middle-aged head librarian, she'd downplayed her looks, and it had become a comfortable façade. Not that she thought there was anything special about the way she looked. As far as she was concerned she was just Miss Average. She didn't really care what others thought of the way she dressed or how she kept her hair up out of her face, but when faced with the denigrating look she'd received from the blonde, she felt totally out of place.

"Alphas," the woman said in a judgmental tone. "Oh goody, a new mate to play with."

"Be very careful, Kirsten. You don't want to bite off more than you can chew." Jonah growled, making Michelle feel sorry for the young woman he was berating. Not that she understood what was going on, but she still felt compassion for the woman. As she stared at Michelle she could see anger and pain in her eyes.

Michelle had no idea what she'd done to get on the woman's bad side. She hadn't even met the woman until she'd come into the library. She watched Kirsten grab a plate of food then storm out of the room without a backward glance. There was a lot more going on here than was on the surface, but she wasn't sure she wanted to know what it was.

"Have you had enough to eat, darlin'?" Jonah's voice broke Michelle from her contemplation.

"Yes. Thank you, Angela. Lunch was lovely," Michelle said as Jonah helped her from her seat and began to lead her from the room. She was surprised when Jonah's brothers, Brock and Mikhail, followed.

"Would you like a tour?" Jonah asked Michelle, sweeping his hand out to encompass the house.

"Yes, thank you. That would be nice. You have a beautiful home," Michelle stated as Jonah led her off the hall to a huge living room.

"Does everyone in the dining room live here?" she asked.

"Yeah, they do. We have a lot of business ventures and most of the people here are family, so it just made sense that we all live together. Besides the house is large enough and we all have our privacy as we all live in different wings of the house," Jonah replied.

"Well, that certainly makes sense."

"How long have you lived in Aztec, baby?" Brock asked from behind her.

Michelle looked over her shoulder to answer Brock and caught him checking out her ass. When he raised his eyes to hers, he gave her a wink and a wicked smile.

"I moved here three weeks ago. I inherited a small cottage from an uncle I didn't even know I had. How those lawyers tracked me down is a mystery. So anyway, I decided to transfer from the library in Mullen to here, so I wouldn't have to pay rent."

"Where does the rest of your family live?" Mikhail asked from her other side.

Michelle turned to him and looked him in the eye. "I don't have any family. I was raised in a convent and in foster homes."

"That explains the uptight façade," Brock muttered behind her.

"Sorry?"

"Don't worry about it, baby, just talking to myself," he replied.

Michelle turned back to Jonah as he took her hand in his and led her through the large living room and to a games room. The room was full of handsome men and a couple of women, including the intrepid Kirsten. The woman shot daggers at her with her eyes. Michelle wondered how she was still standing. She should have keeled over from that glare. Mikhail moved up to her side and placed himself between Kirsten and herself. His back was to her. She had no idea what Mikhail did or said. Even if he had spoken she hadn't heard him, but the next moment Kirsten stormed from the room slamming the door behind her.

"Would you like to see the gardens, Michelle?" Jonah asked, pulling her gaze around to him.

Michelle gave a nod of her head and followed behind as Jonah led her out the side glass sliding doors. Her head was really beginning to pound now and she wanted nothing more than to get in her car and go home, but she sighed and followed the man who, for some reason beyond her comprehension, fascinated her. She wondered why Jonah had asked her out to his house for lunch. To be honest she didn't know what he wanted from her, but was too intrigued by him and his brothers to care.

Michelle was sick and tired of being a good girl. She wanted to let loose and go wild for a while, just to see what the attraction was and how the other half lived. She knew deep down she was different from how she portrayed herself to the world, but she was too scared to let go. She'd never had anyone in her life to really worry about, but she wanted to keep her polite, cool façade in place in case she met someone and they didn't like her true personality. She knew that beneath the front she hid behind, she was a real wild woman, but she kept herself on a tight rein. Deep down Michelle was a closet romantic, believing in the happy endings she knew she would never have the chance to experience.

Michelle knew she was in trouble as soon as the pinpricks of light began to form before her eyes. She'd left her sunglasses in her car, and the sunlight was hurting her eyes, making her head pound even more. She knew what came next. She had to leave now before she disgraced herself by vomiting. She turned away from Jonah and slammed into a hard, warm male body. She squinted as she tried to see whom she'd run into but had to slam her eyes shut when the sunlight penetrated her eyeballs and pierced her skull. Pain knifed through her brain, making her reach up and clutch her head and whimper.

"Are you all right, honey?" Michelle heard Mikhail ask from above her. She couldn't answer. The pain piercing her skull was too bad.

Michelle felt as if every hair follicle on her head was on fire along with her brain, and the numbness began to spread from her forehead down over her nose to her lips. She knew what came next.

"Bathroom quick, now," Michelle managed to say and stumbled. She couldn't help moaning as she was swept up into large, muscular arms, and she felt every step Mikhail took in her head. She knew Jonah and Brock were following behind as their brother rushed her through the house and up the steps. Every step they took echoed loudly in her ears, and then she was being lowered to the floor. He held her on his lap and in his arms as she retched. She was in too much pain to care she wasn't alone, but knew she would feel differently later. She heaved until she had nothing left in her stomach and then slumped back against the comfortable chest behind her. She wanted to rinse her mouth and brush her teeth, crawl into bed and oblivion. Painkillers and sleep were the only way to get rid of her migraine. She felt a cool, damp cloth wipe over her face and mouth, and then a glass was held to her lips. She took a sip of water, rinsed her mouth, and then drank. The sound of Mikhail's quiet voice in her ear made her jerk.

"Do you have any pain medication, honey?"

"Purse, car," Michelle managed to whisper, still clutching at her head.

"I'm on it," she heard Brock say.

Mikhail lifted Michelle into his arms again. He held her against his chest and carried her from the bathroom. She felt a soft mattress beneath her back and the sound of curtains being drawn. More footsteps, then hands were on her, helping her to half sit and half recline. She felt fingers at her lips and opened her mouth for her medication. Two pills were placed on her tongue and a glass of water held to her lips. She took a sip and swallowed them down. The hands helped lower her to the mattress again, and then they were on the buttons of her blouse and skirt. She knew she should protest, but she couldn't remember why. The pain was just too bad, and when she was like this she wouldn't have cared if anyone saw her butt naked.

Her outer clothes were removed, and she could have sworn she heard growls, but couldn't concentrate. She was lucky. The migraine medication worked quickly on her, and she could already feel herself being pulled down to sleep. She didn't fight it. She didn't want to. Even though she was going to feel like she had a hangover when she woke up, she'd rather cope with that than the horrible, excruciating pain. She let go and drifted down into slumber.

* * * *

"Holy mother of…She is hot. It would seem our mate is a closet sex goddess. Would you look at that underwear? She's not as prim and proper as she makes out," Brock said in a voice so low only a werewolf would be able to hear. He stared at their mate's petite, curvy body and the purple lace G-string, matching demi bra, and garter belt.

"Don't just stand their gawking, Brock, help me get the rest of her things off," Mikhail whispered.

"Leave her panties and bra on but remove the garter belt and stockings. We don't want out mate to feel like she's been violated."

Jonah growled as he picked up the medicine bottle and read the contents and the prescription.

"Shit, I hate this. She was in so much pain. When we claim her she won't have to put up with migraines anymore," Jonah stated. "I want to begin trying to seduce our mate sooner than we planned. I can't stand to see her suffer needlessly. Brock, stop staring at her and cover her with a quilt."

Brock did as his brother commanded and reluctantly covered their mate's hot, sexy body. He wanted to crawl on the bed and suckle on her lush breasts. Who knew she would be hiding such a hot little body beneath her conservative, shapeless clothes? He moved to the other side of the bed and shifted Michelle to lie on her side. Then he began to remove the pins from her hair. He gently unwound and untangled her strands until they were flowing down her back, stopping just above her waist. With his better-than-twenty-twenty vision he was able to see the bright red dye streaks of auburn in her brown hair and knew without a doubt there was more to his mate than she showed on the surface. He wanted to keep her here with him and his brothers, to have her by their side and in their beds, to see what the real Michelle was like, but knew she would put up a fight. He looked at his brothers.

"So, what do we do now?"

"We wait until our mate wakes up, and if she wants to go home, we let her go. But we will try and get her to stay here for the rest of the weekend first," Jonah explained.

"How the hell are we going to do that?" Mikhail asked.

"I haven't figured that one out myself yet. If you have any suggestions I'm open to hearing them," Jonah replied.

"The only way I can think of is seducing her," Brock said then held up his hand to placate his brothers' scowls. "I know. We have to wait and make sure she's not in any pain. I'm not that heartless."

"We can't, Brock. As much as I want to agree with you, it's too soon for her. She'd run," Jonah stated.

"I know," Brock said with a sigh. "You can't blame a man for trying though. My wolf is pushing at me to claim her and I know you two are having the same problem, so don't read me the riot act. I just hope we don't have to wait too long. I don't know how long I'll be able to hold him off."

"Come on. Let's leave her to rest. We'll hear when she wakes," Jonah said, moving to the bedroom door, and left without a backward glance.

Brock heard Mikhail follow Jonah. He stood staring down at the pale face of his mate and bit his knuckle. He gave her one last glance and left.

Chapter Five

Oh God. Why did I have to get a migraine here of all places?
Michelle came awake slowly. Her mind was foggy and her stomach a
little queasy, but she sighed in relief when she felt no pain in her
head. She rolled onto her back and slowly opened her eyes. She stared
at the unfamiliar ceiling, gasping out loud as memory slammed into
her mind.

She struggled to sit up and flopped back on the pillows for a
moment, then bolted upright in bed, clutching at the quilt covering
her. She slowly drew a portion of the quilt away from her chest and
looked down. Yep, she was practically naked. *Fuck it.* Whoever had
undressed her would have gotten an eyeful of her sexy lingerie. She
tried to remember who had removed her clothes. She'd had numerous
large hands helping her when she was sick. It could only have been
the three Friess brothers.

Michelle threw the quilt aside and searched for her clothes. She
found them neatly draped over a chair in the corner. She dressed
quickly, and peered out the bedroom door. She sighed in relief when
there was no one about and stepped out into the hallway. She wanted
to get to her car and leave, hopefully without encountering anybody.
She walked along the carpeted hallway, trying to be as quiet as a
mouse, and hesitated at the top of the stairs.

She was halfway down the second level of stairs when she felt
hands push her hard from behind. She flew the rest of the way down.
She tried to grab a hold of the banister, but her hand slipped off. She
had too much momentum to stop herself. Her chest bounced against a
step, and then she was sliding. She reached out with an arm to cushion

her fall as she hurtled to the bottom of the stairs, and when her hand connected with the unforgiving tile floor, her arm bent into an unnatural position. She heard the crack, and agonizing pain radiated up her wrist into her shoulder. She knew she just broken her arm or wrist. She was in too much pain to make a sound. Her breath halted in her lungs and tears tracked down her cheeks as she lay sprawled out on the cold tiled floor.

Gentle hands turned her over, and she couldn't contain the low moan as pain escalated to a new level. She pulled her injured arm slowly into her body and cradled it with the other. She looked up to see Mikhail and Brock standing over her as Jonah picked her up into his arms. She turned her head into his chest, trying to hide her tears as he carried her into the large living room off to the right. She felt sick to her stomach again and prayed like hell she wouldn't throw up all over the man trying to help her.

"Brock, go and get Blayk. I want Michelle checked over. I think she broke her arm. Are you all right, darlin'?" Jonah asked as he sat down on a sofa, taking her with him.

Michelle wanted to get up off his lap, but she was in too much pain to even want to try and move. She nodded her head, her forehead rubbing against his T-shirt-clad chest, too afraid if she opened her mouth she would start screaming and not be able to stop.

She heard the rustle of clothes and knew Blayk was near her. She wanted to be brave and look at him, but she hurt too much.

"I need to get your shirt off, Michelle, so I can give you a shot for the pain. Can you sit up for me?" an unfamiliar male voice asked.

Michelle lifted her head and then her upper body from her slumped position on Jonah's chest. She looked up and saw Blayk looking down at her, a worried frown on his face. She lifted her good arm and began to slowly undo the buttons on her blouse. When she fumbled a few times, Jonah brushed her hand away and took over the task. Once done, he helped ease her good arm out of her sleeve and carefully pulled her back against his chest.

She felt and smelled as Blayk swabbed her arm with disinfectant then felt a slight prick as he gave her the pain medication. She reacted quickly to meds and felt her limbs become heavy and as if she were floating as the medication began to work. She couldn't prevent the giggle bubbling up in her chest from escaping her mouth as Jonah lifted her up and turned her around on his lap. She flinched with pain as Blayk began to examine her arm as he talked to Jonah. She could hear what he was saying but had a little trouble comprehending his words.

"You could have this fixed by tomorrow if you and your brothers claimed her, Alpha. If you don't she'll be wearing a cast for at least six weeks. She'll need help for the first few days. She's going to be in too much pain to cope on her own."

"Wh–Whatsh an alpha?" Michelle slurred then giggled.

"It seems our mate can't handle pain meds. I wonder what she's like when she's had alcohol," Michelle heard Brock say.

"Brock!" Michelle heard Jonah and Mikhail say at the same time and giggled again.

"I'm not deaf, you know," Michelle slurred.

"We know you aren't, baby," Brock replied.

"Why d–do you all keep calling me that?"

"What, darlin'?" Jonah asked.

"That. Darlin', baby, that stuff?" Michelle asked.

"Because we like calling you endearments," Jonah answered. "Michelle, I want you to listen to me and not interrupt until I've finished, all right?"

"Okay."

"We are all werewolves, darlin', and you are our mate. If we claim you by biting you, our saliva will change your DNA and you'll heal much faster. You won't be able to shift shape like we do, but all your senses and healing ability will work so much better. I can get Blayk to put a cast on your arm if you wish, but if you choose the cast you'll be staying here so we can help you. Or we could bite you and by tomorrow your arm will be healed," Jonah stated.

"You're fucking shitting me," Michelle got out around her uncooperative tongue, and then burst out laughing. She should have known something was up with Jonah and his brothers. Why should she find a sane man who was attracted to her? No one else had ever bothered with a second look to see what was beneath the surface. He had to be crazy to believe the nonsense he was spouting. "You are fucking crazy if you think I am going to believe that crap. I knew this was too good to be true."

"I am telling you the truth, darlin'. I know it must be hard for you to comprehend normally, let alone when you're doped up on pain meds, but I am being truthful with you. Brock, show her," Jonah commanded.

"And there she is." Brock's voice drew her gaze to his.

Michelle gasped and covered her mouth with her hand as Brock began to strip his clothes from his body. His tight T-shirt came off first, and she let her eyes rove over his dark, tanned skin, his muscles rippling as he moved. His hands went to down to his pants, and he popped the button then lowered the zipper. He pushed his jeans down over her thick, muscular thighs, and she couldn't help but snap her gaze back up to his crotch. The man wasn't wearing any underwear, and his half-hard cock was huge as it hung between his legs. She licked her dry lips and watched as his penis twitched and began to fill with more blood. The sound of his voice had her eyes snapping back up to his.

"You're killing me, baby."

"What are you doing?" Michelle whispered, and then swallowed loudly.

"I'm showing you it's true. We are all werewolves and you are our mate." Brock reiterated what Jonah had told her.

Oh God. They were all delusional. Michelle watched Brock as he moved into the center of the room, totally confident with his own nudity. His now fully engorged cock bobbed and swayed as he moved. The man's appendage was every bit as large as the rest of him. It was nearly as thick as her wrist and reached up to his navel. The air around him began to blur and shimmer. The sound of bones cracking and joints popping as his muscles shifted and his body contorted was sickening. She felt bile rise in her throat and swallowed. Her breath was panting out of her mouth, and she gave a scared whimper as Brock dropped to the ground on all fours. His spine rippled as his back arched, a tail forming at the end of his backbone as fur erupted from his skin and covered his body. She pushed herself back into Jonah's embrace as the wolf who had been Brock moved toward her. She felt Jonah wrap his arms around her waist, holding her securely as the wolf stopped inches from her legs. He was huge. He towered above her while she sat on Jonah's lap. She stared into his eyes and looked away, scared she was challenging him as he stood tall before her. She jerked when his cool, wet nose nudged her hand, then groaned in pain since she'd jolted her broken arm. She looked back down to her hands as Brock rubbed his face over her good hand and couldn't resist reaching out to stroke him.

She was surprised at how soft his fur was. She'd expected it to feel coarse like a dog's fur, but it was soft and silky beneath her touch. She threaded her fingers through the strands then reached up and scratched behind his ear. He groaned with pleasure and leaned his head to the side, giving her easier access. She felt electricity pulse around him as he moved back from her touch, and she watched the horrible contortions his body went through as he changed back. It took a matter of seconds before he stood before her naked once more. She sighed with relief as he began to pull his clothes back on, covering his delectable nakedness from her eyes.

"Fucking hell, you really are werewolves," Michelle said as she tried to push off of Jonah's lap, but he wouldn't let her, and since she only had the use of one arm, she gave up the futile action.

"Yes we are, darlin'," Jonah replied needlessly.

"How is this possible? What do you mean I'm your mate? Who is 'we?'?" Michelle rattled off quickly, her words blending together.

"Mikhail, Brock, and I are all your mates, and we were born as werewolves. We are the same as you, darlin', just with different DNA. We have a…little more than a human being," Jonah explained. "Now, you have a choice. Do you want us to bite you so you can heal faster, or do you want Blayk here, who is a doctor I might add, to put a cast on your arm? Think carefully, Michelle. If you have a cast put on, you will be staying here until it comes off again. And if you choose to let us claim you, you'll be moving in here permanently."

"What sort of choice is that? No fucking way am I letting you and your brothers bite me. I'll have the cast and then I'll be leaving. You can't keep me here against my will."

"You're right, we can't. But think about how you'll cope by yourself with a cast on your arm. You're going to need help, darlin'," Jonah declared as he bent his head and licked the side of her neck.

Michelle felt her pussy spasm, and cream leaked out of her sex to dampen her panties. *How the hell can these men turn my once sleeping libido, to a raging flame so quickly?* She wanted to give in and let them claim her, bite her. The thought of having sex with three men at once had her body heating so hot, it was a wonder her blood wasn't boiling. But everything she'd learned from the nuns at the convent whispered through her mind. She just couldn't do it. She couldn't take the chance and risk her true personality breaking free. If she did, she was scared she would never get her front back under control.

"Please put the cast on," Michelle said as she looked up at Blayk.

"I'll need you in the dining room. That way when I slop plaster on the floor, Angela won't read me the riot act."

"All right," Michelle replied, trying to get off Jonah's lap, but he wouldn't let her.

Jonah moved her back on his lap, and she felt his hard cock digging into her hip. She tried to squirm away, but he moved an arm beneath her knees, the other around her shoulders, being careful not to injure her arm, and stood with graceful ease. Then he was carrying her into the dining room.

He held her on his lap as Blayk gathered his supplies from a large cupboard off the side of the kitchen and she tried to regulate her rapid breathing.

"How did you fall down the stairs, honey?" Mikhail asked as he pulled up a chair and sat down close to her and Jonah.

"Uh, I don't remember," Michelle answered.

"Are you lying to me?" Mikhail asked as he grasped her chin between a finger and thumb, turning her head toward him.

"Uh…"

"Don't try and lie to me again, honey. I'm a werewolf, remember, I can smell it when you're lying."

Fuck. Now what do I do? Michelle knew damn well she hadn't slipped and she would bet on her life she knew who had pushed her, but she didn't want to get the woman in trouble.

She knew the woman had been nasty to her, but she had seen the underlying pain in the other woman's eyes and didn't want to cause her any more grief. She had finally worked out that Kirsten had feelings for Jonah, Mikhail, and Brock. She had remembered what the woman had said to her in the library, and she had felt angry and sorry for Kirsten on her behalf. No female deserved to be treated like a sex object. If she knew the Friess brothers a little better she might have already given them a tongue lashing, but she would bide her time and give it when the opportunity arose.

Well, the only thing she could think of in her defense was to say nothing at all. She pulled her chin from Mikhail's grasp, compressed her lips tight across her teeth, and refused to answer. She sighed, relieved when Blayk pushed Mikhail out of his seat and commandeered it for himself. Saved by the bell, metaphorically speaking.

Blayk worked on her arm, soaking the strips of plaster in a bowl of water, then wrapping it around her limb. By the time he was finished, she had plaster covering her palm around her thumb, over her knuckles, to just below her elbow. The plaster was still damp, and she shivered as goose bumps rose on her flesh. She watched as Blayk cleaned up his mess, came back to check she had enough room in her plaster in case of swelling, then left the room without a backward glance. She covered her mouth to stifle a yawn. The pain medication was making her drowsy. At least she wasn't slurring her words anymore. She hoped.

"You need a nap. When you wake up, we will have the answers we want, Michelle. I'm not letting you get away without telling us what happened. And I suggest you think about telling the truth," Jonah stated firmly as he scooped her up in his arms once more.

Arrogant asshole. Who does he think he is, ordering me about? I'm not one of his minions to follow along without question. She knew he was the leader of their group. She had ascertained that information easily enough throughout the day, by the way the others in the house seemed to defer to him. *I'll show him he can't walk all over me.*

Chapter Six

Michelle groaned with frustration when she realized she'd fallen asleep. She'd had no intention of doing so. She had actually planned on waiting until she was alone, and then she was going to try and slip out of the large mansion-style house unnoticed. She had no idea what time it was but knew it was dark outside. The curtains in the room had a small gap in the middle, and she saw it was pitch black outside. A small lamp on the bedside table offered muted light for her to see by.

She sat up, groaned as her newly casted arm protested at the movement, threw the covers back on the bed, and swung her legs over the side. She dropped her head in her good hand when she realized she was only wearing her panties and a large white T-shirt. She wouldn't be able to put her own shirt back on because she didn't know where it was and she knew the sleeve wouldn't fit over her cast. She looked around for her skirt but couldn't find that either. A toweling robe was lying across the end of the bed, so she picked it up, carefully slid it over the cast, and then struggled to get her good arm into the other sleeve. She looked around for her flat slip-on shoes

Michelle crept along the dimly lit hallway and then slowly descended the stairs. She kept a good grip on the banister this time, but she kept checking over her shoulder to make sure no one snuck up on her and pushed her down. She hesitated at the bottom of the stairs, listening to the rumble of masculine voices coming from the dining room. She figured it must be around dinnertime, but since she slept most of the day away and she was still in a bit of pain, she wasn't hungry at all. Instead of turning right into the kitchen dining room, she turned left into the massive living room. She was relieved to find it empty. She walked into the room and sat down in the corner of the large sofa, her arm cradled against her chest because it was hurting something fierce. She curled her legs beneath her and rested her back against the arm and back of the sofa.

She let her mind drift and wondered what it would be like to have so many people, family, around all the time. Of course she'd been around a lot of people in the convent and small families in foster care, but she'd never really felt as if she fit in. Then her mind jumped, and she gasped as she remembered Jonah telling her that they were all werewolves. She knew she'd laughed at him, and she remembered swearing. *Shit.* She let part of her true personality surface, while under the influence of drugs. The blurry image of Brock stripping down to his glorious skin and then changing into a wolf before her eyes flashed through her mind. She rose to her feet in agitation. She had to get out of here. She didn't care that she was only covered in a T-shirt and robe. She was leaving. She could still drive but with only one hand on the wheel, which would be dangerous, but she would manage.

Michelle ran to the door of the living room and cautiously peeked out around the jamb. When she saw no one, she quickly ran toward the exit she remembered Jonah leading her through when they'd first arrived. She kept her footsteps light and was pleased when she made it to the doorway without being caught. She reached out for the handle with her good arm and turned the knob.

"Where do you think you're off to?" Mikhail growled in her ear.

Michelle screamed and jumped about a foot off the floor. She spun around, her heart racing and thudding in her chest. She placed her good hand on her chest, trying to stop her heart from pounding.

"I...um...Look, you can't keep me here. I want to go home," Michelle said, raising her chin at him. She was getting a crick in her neck as she glared up at him and had to lower her head to ease the ache.

"Jonah gave you a choice, honey. He told you if you didn't let us claim you and you chose to have the cast put on, you would need to stay here so we can help you," Mikhail reminded her.

"You can tell me what to do all you like, but I don't know you or your brothers. I think it would be best if I went home."

"I don't," Mikhail replied. "Look at me, Michelle."

Michelle automatically responded to Mikhail's command, then berated herself for doing so without putting up a fight. The heat she could see in his silver-gray eyes as he stared at her was enough to singe her hair. She felt her breasts swell and her nipples harden. Her clit began to ache, and her pussy throbbed. She felt her cunt release a well of cream and felt her panties becoming wet.

"I can smell your need, honey. We could give you relief if you'd only let us."

"What?" Michelle asked. She nearly groaned at how breathy her question sounded, even to her own ears. She stepped back as Mikhail moved in closer to her, and her back thudded against the door behind her and the door handle dug into her flesh. She moved to the side, trying to see a way around Mikhail. She wanted to run, but the fire in her body prevented her from moving. She stared into Mikhail's eyes as he leaned down toward her.

Michelle's whimper sounded loud even to her own ears. She wanted to reach up and push him away, but she also wanted to grab hold of him and lay her lips on his. Her mind was at war with her body. His face was only inches away from hers, and she could feel his breath on her forehead. He reached out to her and drew her up against the length of his body. The top of her head only reached his collarbone. She had never felt so small and fragile. He wrapped one of his muscular arms around her waist and placed a hand beneath her ass. He lifted her up until they were face-to-face. She stared into his eyes and saw his pupils dilate. His breathing was as choppy as her own, both racing in and out from between their lips. He pulled her in closer, and she felt the huge bulge at his crotch against her thigh. She tried to wriggle away, but he held her fast.

Michelle heard him groan as he moved the last few inches and covered her mouth with his own. She tried to keep her body stiff using all her concentration, but her natural instinct won and she found herself wrapping her arms around his neck and her legs around his waist. He licked along the seam of her lips with his tongue, making her whimper with desire. She opened her mouth to him and moaned into his mouth as he slid his tongue between her teeth. He swept into her mouth, tasting and exploring every inch of her moist depths. She gave herself over to him as fire raced through her veins.

Michelle felt her back connect with the door behind her and mewled as Mikhail curled his tongue around hers, drawing the muscle from her mouth into his own. The feel of his lips closing around her tongue and sucking made her rock her hips against his belly. The friction of her wet panties sliding between them was so good, she didn't want to stop. Mikhail released her tongue and swept his tongue along the inside of her cheeks, over her teeth, and to the roof of her mouth. She threaded her fingers through the silky strands of his hair and groaned as he withdrew his tongue to nibble on her bottom lip then slowly licked and kissed his way along her jawline to her ear. She thrust her hips against him and whimpered as he pushed his tongue into her ear, sending shivers of need racing up and down her spine.

She could feel cream leaking from her slick folds, her panties now soaking wet as he moved his mouth to gently nip on her earlobe. She felt him shift beneath her arms, and his body arched as he pulled her crotch against his own. He grasped her hips and helped her to rub herself over his hard cock, bulging beneath his jeans. He humped her, slamming his groin into hers as she rocked her cunt up and down. Her womb was heavy with desire, her clit aching with need, and her pussy clenching open and closed. She was coiled as tight as a bowstring and only he could give her relief. He pressed his cock into her crotch hard one last time, and she screamed. She threw her head back, making a loud thud as the back of her head connected with the door, her liquid release making her body jerk and shiver as wave after wave of ecstasy washed over her.

She clung to him and buried her face in his neck. She couldn't believe what she had just done. Her broken wrist was throbbing like a bitch, and she was too shocked by what had just happened to look at him. She clung to him tighter as he tried to draw her away from him.

"You have nothing to be ashamed of, honey. It's natural for mates to want to fuck. It's only going to get more intense as we spend more time with each other," Mikhail advised.

Michelle sighed and slowly released her hold around his neck. The pain in her arm was so intense now she was beginning to feel ill. She pulled her injured arm against her chest and cradled it with her good one. Her back and ass were still against the door behind her, and only Mikhail's arms kept her from sliding down. She caught movement off to her right and turned her head. She met Jonah's and Brock's eyes as they stared at her. The fire in them had her libido twitching to life again, but the pain in her arm tamped it down.

"That was so fucking hot," Brock said, his voice a deep, garbled growl.

Michelle felt her cheeks heat with embarrassment and lowered her eyes.

"Please, let me down," Michelle demanded and was relieved when Mikhail released her ass, moving his hands to her hips. She lowered her legs and wobbled slightly as her now-weak limbs protested against her weight. Mikhail held her steady until she placed a hand on his chest and pushed. Thankfully he stepped back away from her, and she sagged against the door.

"I would really like to go home now," Michelle whispered.

"No," Jonah responded. "I can't let you go when you're in so much pain, darlin'. You're going to need help, and the only way we can do that is if you stay here. Of course, we could all come and stay at your place if you'd prefer?"

"No!" Michelle screeched then cleared her throat. "No, I don't have the room."

"Then it looks like you'll be staying here with us. If you give me your house keys, I can have Cindy taken over to collect some clothes for you. Oh, by the way, you're not working until that cast comes off."

"What? No, you can't do that. I have bills to pay, I need the money. I don't have enough sick leave accrued to be taking time off," Michelle protested as she glared at Jonah.

"Don't worry, darlin', you'll still get paid. You were injured in my house after all, and we will get back to that in a moment. I will have one of the Omegas fill in at the library for you. Now, come on into the living room. You're as white as a sheet and look about ready to fall down. Mikhail will carry you," Jonah commanded in a low, gravelly voice, and Michelle saw him glare at his brother.

"I don't need to be carried. I can walk," Michelle protested as Mikhail lifted her into his arms and cradled her against his chest. "What the hell is an Omega?"

"I know you can, honey, but once a command is given it's carried out or there will be hell to pay. There are three levels to a wolf pack, Michelle. The Alpha or Alphas in our case. Next are the Betas and then the Omegas. An Alpha is the leader of a pack, which is what Jonah, Brock, and I are. Jonah is the most senior Alpha of our pack since he is the eldest, and what he says is law. When he puts his foot down everyone has to obey. He can even use a compulsion in his voice to get someone reluctant to obey, to comply.

"Betas are second in line to the Alphas. They usually deal with the safety of the Alphas and the rest of the pack. The Omegas are the lower level of pack members, but no less significant than the rest of us. We all live here, together in a den, this house. Wolves like to stay together. We don't like being separated from our family.

"Jonah's not happy with me at the moment because I've made your arm ache." Mikhail sighed.

"But it wasn't your entire fault," Michelle whispered and looked up at Mikhail.

"I'm glad you aren't putting all the blame on me, honey, but let me take the heat for the both of us. When Jonah goes all Alpha male he can be a bit overbearing."

"No shit," Michelle replied with a grin.

The sight of Mikhail winking at her and his loud laugh went straight to her crotch. *Oh fuck. I'm in trouble.*

Chapter Seven

Jonah was already seated on the large sofa when Mikhail carried their mate into the living room. The sight of her pale face and the pinched, pained look around her lips had him growling in frustration. He knew one bite from him and his brothers would begin the healing process immediately. That their mate was so stubborn had him admiring and cursing her at the same time. He waited until Mikhail sat beside him, sitting with Michelle on his lap. He noticed Brock move away from the mantle, and then his brother sat on the other side of their mate. She was pushing against Mikhail's shoulder with her good hand, trying to get him to let her go. Mikhail finally relented and placed her on the seat beside him. Jonah had to bite his tongue when she gave his brother a glare, so he wouldn't burst out laughing.

Jonah turned, angling his body toward Michelle, and held in the smile he felt forming as she glared at him, too. Their little mate was full of fire. She had a wild side she kept hidden from everyone around her, as well as herself. He knew she wouldn't be able to maintain the façade she put up around him and his brothers for long. He couldn't wait until she let her true personality shine through. He reached out and clasped her small chin between his thumb and finger, holding her gaze to his.

"You need to tell us how you fell down the stairs, darlin'. And don't you dare try and bullshit me. I can smell it when you're lying," Jonah stated firmly.

"Someone pushed me," Michelle snapped.

"Who?" Jonah demanded.

"I don't know. I didn't see anyone. I was too busy trying to stop my fall."

"But you have an idea, just like I do," Jonah said. "Kirsten, come here now."

Jonah knew Michelle felt the power behind his demand. She shivered and jerked her chin out of his hold. He put so much force behind his command, there was no way in hell a werewolf could have denied him, let alone a human.

He caught the scent of Kirsten's fear before she was even in the room. When she was finally standing before him, her head lowered in supplication, he stood up and moved closer to her. He sniffed at her, the scent of her fear rolling off her in waves. He stood before her and waited for her to look up at him.

"Did you push my mate down the stairs?" Jonah roared the question and knew every *were* on the property would have heard him.

Jonah sighed when Kirsten whimpered instead of answering. He knew damn well she had been the one to hurt his mate. His beast was pushing against him, wanting him to change and rip her throat out. He took a few deep breaths and let them out slowly, once more in control of his wolf. He reached out and took Kirsten's hand in his, lifted it to his nose, and sniffed. The lingering scent of his mate was still on her skin. He dropped her hands and stepped back.

"You will pack your bags and leave immediately. I will give you one month's severance pay and you will never set foot on this land again. If I or any of the others catch you on my land, you will be terminated. Is that understood?"

"Alpha, please, I didn't mean…"

"Get out of my sight before I kill you *now*," Jonah yelled. He sighed as Kirsten rushed from the room, sobbing and whimpering. He turned back and looked at his mate. He expected to see fear on her face. Boy, was he surprised. He could see and smell fury pouring off her in waves. She pushed against Mikhail's arm, and he let her go.

She stood up and sauntered over to him. She smacked her good hand onto his chest.

"I can't believe you did that? Do you have no compassion? Don't you realize that woman has feelings for you? What did you do to her? Fuck her and then dump her? How could you be so heartless? If anyone is to blame for my injury it's you and your brothers. You will go and apologize to that woman, right now. She told me you were together before I came onto the scene. You will go and apologize right now for the way you have treated her and tell her she can stay here in her home for as long as she likes. She will apologize to me after you and your brothers have redeemed yourselves with her. Fucking men, I can't believe how you all treat women."

Jonah was astounded by his fiery mate railing at him. She'd slapped at his chest countless times in her rant, and her cheeks were now a rosy pink, her breathing and her eyes full of passion. He stood there staring at her like a dumb-ass. She turned away from him, and he snagged her around the waist, pulling her back against the front of his body.

"You are the perfect Alpha's mate, darlin'. I can't believe you stood up to me, and of course you're right. We could have handled Kirsten a lot better than we did. You have no idea what you've just done, but you'll find out soon enough," Jonah whispered into her ear, then nibbled on the top of it. "Brock, Mikhail, go and prepare a bath for our mate. Michelle will be sleeping in our bed tonight."

"I most certainly will not," Michelle said haughtily.

Jonah grinned against her head. Their mate was trying to be cool and haughty again. It had his hard cock throbbing against the zipper of his jeans.

"Yes, you will, darlin'. And don't you dare tell me you don't want to. I can smell your pussy from here."

"Well, I never…"

"I know, darlin'. I promise we'll go easy on you the first time." Jonah growled and released her. "Take her up to our suite. Kirsten, come here."

Jonah watched as his brothers pulled a reluctant Michelle from the room and waited for Kirsten. He prowled the room, eager to get this over with so he could join his brothers and mate in their rooms. He heard Kirsten's slow, reluctant footsteps and turned toward the door. She stood just inside the doorway, her head lowered, and she was gripping her hands so hard her knuckles were white.

"It seems I owe you an apology. I am sorry for the way my brothers and I used you. I know you think yourself to be in love with us, but that isn't the case. When you find your mate, you will know what we had was just sex. It won't even compare to what you think you feel toward us. I am willing to let you stay here, in your home, but if I hear you have tried to harm my mate in any way again, you will be banished. You can thank my mate for my change of heart. She made me see reason, she made me aware of the way we had treated you, and for that I'm sorry. You will of course apologize to my mate when you see her next, for hurting her."

"Thank you, Alpha," Kirsten sobbed and rushed over to him. She knelt at his knees and rubbed her face over his jeans. "I won't let you down. I promise. I will certainly apologize to your mate."

"See that you do. You may leave," Jonah stated and watched as Kirsten stood up, bowed to him, and hurried away.

"You have no idea how you just accepted the role of being our mate, Michelle, even if it wasn't a conscious thought," Jonah muttered to himself. He felt a grin spread over his face and hurried from the room. He was eager to claim his mate.

Chapter Eight

Jonah opened the door to their suite of rooms and inhaled the scent of his mate mixing with his and his brothers' scents. His cock throbbed, and his balls ached. His wolf was pushing at him again to claim Michelle, and he didn't know if he would be able to hold his beast back much longer. He heard the sound of water splashing and knew his mate was naked in his bathroom, in his bath. He closed the door quietly behind him and walked toward the adjoining bathroom. He took in her warm, pink, moist flesh as she leaned against the back of the tub. Her hair was up on top of her head, her cast covered in a plastic bag resting against the rim of the tub. Her eyes were closed and her cheeks were a rosy red. The sound of her voice drew him into the room.

"I don't want you in here with me while I'm naked, Brock, Mikhail. I can bathe myself, you know. I have been doing it for a long time. I wish you'd leave me alone."

"Not gonna happen, baby," Brock replied.

"We don't want to risk you slipping and hurting your arm," Mikhail advised.

"You have accepted us as your mates, Michelle. We're not leaving you alone." Jonah growled as he looked down at his mate's naked body.

She was perfection. She was so tiny, but her breasts were lush and full, her waist small enough he would be able to span it with his hands, and her hips were nice and curvy. He wanted to scoop her up, lay her on the bed, and plunge his cock into her wet heat. He was surprised that she wasn't trying to hide her assets from view. He moved to the end of the tub, squatted at the side, and picked up her delicate foot. He reached for the bath gel and poured a little on top of her foot and began to wash her. He made sure he kneaded the tight muscles in her sole and couldn't prevent his eyes from taking a leisurely stroll up her soft, shapely legs until they reached the juncture of her thighs. He bit down on his tongue as he saw her bare pussy lips peeking from between her thighs. Even though he could have peeked at her when she was in her G-string earlier, he had restrained himself in deference to her feelings. Their mate wasn't the conservative prude she portrayed. His slid his hands from her foot and up her calf. She slipped through his fingers when she jerked her leg out of his hand.

"I did not accept you as my mates. Where do you get that insane idea from?"

Jonah reached for her leg again and smiled when she pulled her knees up, taking her limbs from his reach. She could fight them all she wanted, but she had accepted her fate when she stood toe-to-toe with him as an Alpha's mate would.

"You argued with me about Kirsten's punishment. Only an Alpha's mate would do such a thing. You accepted us without even realizing what you were doing."

"Well, there's a clue for you, buddy. I had no idea I would be accepting you as my mates if I stood up for a fellow human being. I would do the same for anyone in need. So you can just, just, fuck off."

"Yes, I will fuck and so will you. We are going to claim you, Michelle, and you are going to let us."

"I will not," Michelle replied indignantly, crossing her arms over her chest.

"Ah, but you will, darlin'. Get her out and dry her off," Jonah commanded.

"Look, just leave, all of you. I can dry myself."

"Not gonna happen, baby," Brock replied.

Jonah stood off to the side and watched as his brothers hauled their mate from the large tub. He was pleased they were careful of her injured arm, and that she stood still as they took care of her. His brothers had her dried off and wrapped in a large towel. She surprised him by staying silent and not cussing at them some more. It seemed their mate wasn't as averse to them claiming her as she liked to voice.

Mikhail scooped Michelle off her feet and left the bathroom, and Jonah followed behind. His brother gently placed their mate onto the massive bed in the master bedroom and whipped the towel off her body. Michelle tried to scramble off the other side of the bed, but since she only had the use of one arm, she was finding the task difficult.

Jonah heard her laugh and looked up to see her passion-glazed eyes staring at him and his brothers. She surprised him once more when she spoke.

"Bring it on!"

Jonah crawled up onto the bottom of the bed and clasped his hand around one of her ankles. She kicked out at him, giving him an enticing view of her pink, wet vagina, and he knew she was just as aroused as he and his brothers were. She laughed again and tried to give him another playful kick. He pulled on her leg and slid her back into the center of the mattress, careful not to hurt her. He removed his hand from her ankle and placed both his hands on her hips. He slid his legs to the outside of her thighs and caged her in. He leaned forward, virtually covering her with his body, and took her mouth with his.

Jonah used his lips to pry her mouth open and swept his tongue inside. The taste of her, his mate, was more than he had ever thought possible. He couldn't get enough. He swirled and parried his tongue against hers, then nipped her bottom lip with his teeth. The sound of her moans had him thrusting his tongue back into her depths for another taste of her. She was pure female. He could taste her desire on his tongue and fanned the flames even higher by drawing her tongue into his mouth and sucking on it. She arched her breasts up into his chest and began to rub her nipples over his T-shirt. He growled his approval and slid his mouth over her face, kissing every inch of her soft, delectable skin as he went. He licked down the side of her neck and inhaled her pulse point.

He felt his canine teeth elongate, and he knew he couldn't have stopped even if he wanted to. Not that he did. He bit into her flesh, his canines sinking into her neck where it met her shoulder as he gripped her writhing hips. His mate threw her head back and screamed her pleasure. Even though this was the first time he had ever claimed a mate, he'd heard the stories from his elders that the claiming bite only ever gave pleasure. It seemed that was true. Her body jerked as she climaxed beneath him from his mark. He withdrew his teeth, licked the wound clean of blood, and raised his head.

She was so beautiful in the throes of orgasm, he was in danger of shooting off in his pants. He grabbed her hair, released it from the elastic she'd bound it in to bathe, and wrapped it around his fist. He tilted her head toward him, took her mouth beneath his, and devoured her. He was lost. He knew he would never get enough of her no matter how many times he had her. He withdrew his mouth from hers and got off the bed. He needed to let his brothers mark her, and then they were all going to fuck her.

Jonah began to strip his clothes off as he watched Brock get on the bed at her side and pull her naked body against his tall, solid frame. She was so small compared to his oversized brother. She looked so fragile. Jonah barked out a laugh as Michelle grabbed at Brock's hair with her good hand and pulled his mouth down to hers. Their little mate was a totally wild woman. She attacked Brock's mouth like a starving woman, and maybe she was. She'd grown up in a convent and numerous foster homes. She'd never had the love and affection of a real family. She'd probably never had many hugs. That thought saddened Jonah to no end. To imagine this woman, his mate, as a child, never misbehaving for fear of being sent packing made pain pierce his heart.

Jonah heard Michelle scream as Brock bit into her on the opposite side of her neck to where he had. The sight of her in the ecstasy of another climax was nearly more than he could stand. He wanted to sink into her wet, tight cunt, now. When Brock eased back from Michelle, he urged Mikhail to hurry up.

"Mikhail, claim her now, I can't hold out," Jonah told his brother telepathically.

Mikhail didn't answer Jonah. His brother growled at him and pushed Brock off their mate, off to her side. Jonah climbed onto the bed at the bottom as Mikhail lay at her other side. Mikhail pulled his mate's back into the curve of his now-naked body, and Jonah heard him inhale her scent. He licked over the top of her shoulder, and Jonah could see his canines elongating. Then his brother opened his mouth and slid his canines in deep. She thrashed against Mikhail's body and she climaxed yet again as his sibling marked her. She was theirs. No one could take her away from them, not even another werewolf. They would be able to find her if she was within close range, any time. Her DNA was etched into their blood as theirs was now etched into hers.

Their unique *were* powers would be more enhanced now, and they would be able to communicate with Michelle telepathically over time. They also wouldn't want to be away from their mate for any extended length of time. Once mated he and his brothers would want to make love with Michelle often and have her by their side constantly. If she ever left them they would suffer a slow, agonizing death and they would leave a pack behind without any direction. Jonah saw Brock rise to his feet and shred his clothes from his body. It was obvious he was in a frenzy of need just like he and Mikhail were. Brock climbed back onto the bed, and he and Mikhail helped their mate over onto her back, mindful of her injured arm. Jonah reached out and grasped her ankles in his hands and spread her legs. She tried to thwart him, but she wasn't strong enough. He slid the palms of his hands up the inside of her calves and the silky skin of her thighs. He gently pried her legs wider, moved his nose closer to her cunt, and breathed deeply. Her musky scent called to him, and he lowered his head between her thighs.

Jonah slid his tongue into her creamy flesh and licked her from top to bottom. The taste of her cream sliding over his tongue made him growl into her flesh, then he stabbed his tongue into her tight cunt hole to gather more. He swallowed her essence as he lapped and twirled his longer *were-tongue* into the depths of her sheath. She was salty and sweet, and he knew he could spend hours eating out her pussy. The sounds she made as he made love to her with his mouth only heightened his need for more. He opened his eyes as he slid his tongue up through her delicate folds and flicked her clit as he saw his brothers sucking on her nipples. He couldn't see her face because her neck was arched, pushing her head further into the pillow she was resting on.

Jonah sucked her clit into his mouth and pushed one of his fingers into her tight, wet heat. Her vaginal walls rippled around his digit, which had him at the brink of his control. He eased his mouth away from her cunt, withdrew his finger, and moved his body into a sitting position between her splayed thighs. He grabbed the base of his hard cock in his hand and pumped it a few times, before he aimed for her small hole. Her flesh enveloped the head of his cock, and it was pure nirvana. He heard her whimper and knew she was having trouble adjusting to his size, so he reached for her clit and began to massage the small bundle of nerves with his thumb. He groaned as her skin stretched and her muscles relaxed enough for the tip of his rod to slide into her sheath. He held still, letting his mate become accustomed to the intrusion, all the while lightly massaging her clit.

He began to pump his hips, only moving in small, shallow thrusts but gaining a little more depth each time. His brothers were taking turns devouring her mouth and nipples, keeping her arousal at its highest level without pushing her over the edge. He slid in more and more, his thrusting hips taking his cock deeper with every slide and glide in and out of her flesh. He froze when he felt his cock hit her tight muscles and looked down to their joined flesh to see he was only halfway in his mate's body. He let out a howl of possessiveness and joy, knowing for a fact his mate had never been with another man. He had suspected as much by her uptight persona but hadn't really known for sure. Until now.

Jonah carefully slid his legs beneath Michelle's and pulled her thighs wide. He moved his body over hers and shoved his brothers to the side. She looked up at him, her eyes glazed with passion, her lips swollen from his brothers' kisses, and her nipples moist and hard. He lowered his head to hers and gave her a kiss so carnal they both went up in flames. He held her hips still between his hands as he kissed her, slid his cock head to the entrance of her cunt, and slowly slid back in all the way. He didn't stop, capturing his mate's small whimper of discomfort in his mouth, and then froze when he was embedded balls-deep in her tight, rippling cunt.

Jonah released her mouth and stared down into her eyes. When she shifted beneath him with a wiggle of her hips and moaned at the sensation, he couldn't hold still for another moment. He eased his cock from her body until just his head was inside her, and then he pushed back in. With every slide and glide of his cock in and out of her tight, wet cunt, he slowly increased the pace. It wasn't long before he could feel his balls slapping against her ass as he thrust in and out of her body. He slid his hands beneath her ass and lifted her hips up into his as he taught her his rhythm. She caught on quickly, and instead of him pulling her into him, he began to knead the globes of her ass as she met him thrust for thrust. He could feel her internal muscles fluttering along the length of his hard shaft and knew she was close. He slammed his hips into hers, making sure he contacted with her clit with each thrust. He growled long and low in his chest as his mate's cunt clamped down on his cock, the feel of her liquid release on his flesh making him pump faster.

He thrust two, three, four more times, threw his head back, and howled as he emptied his seed into her body. He held still, gripping her hips firmly until the last of his load spewed from the end of his cock. He collapsed down on her but braced his weight on his arms, careful not to crush her. He kissed her long and hard then withdrew his cock and mouth from her at the same time. He rolled to the side of her, inadvertently knocking Mikhail off the edge of the bed. The sound of his brother growling as his ass hit the floor sent him into roars of laughter. He was so happy, he felt as if he could take on the world and win. He turned his head to the side to see Michelle staring at him in wonder. She was obviously surprised he did indeed have a sense of humor.

He fell in love with her there and then. He knew he would never be able to survive without his mate by his side and had no intention of doing so.

Chapter Nine

Michelle couldn't believe she'd just had sex. Had just given her virginity away as if it was nothing. To see Jonah laughing like a loon beside her made her feel uncomfortable, because she wasn't sure if he was laughing at her or if it was because she hadn't put up much of a fight. She had goaded Jonah into making love with her, practically begged with her body for him to take her. She had feelings for these three men, but didn't want to. They had wormed their way into her heart before she knew they were there. She was so stupid. She should have left when she'd had the chance. She had given away her body as well as her heart.

She felt tears well up and knew she was going to cry. She hated to cry in front of anyone. She blinked a few times, trying to keep the moisture welling in her eyes at bay, but that only made the tears spill over and run down her cheeks. She surged up onto her feet on the mattress, jumped over the top of Brock, and landed on the floor with a thud. She stumbled but was relieved she stayed upright and ran to the bathroom. She slammed the door behind her, the lock snicking into place. She turned on the shower and got in under the steaming water, heedless of the plaster cast on her arm. The first sob hit hard, taking her to her knees. She wrapped her arms around her body and then laughed hysterically at the once-firm cast on her arm. It was now a soggy mass of goop, dripping down into the base of the shower. Her arm wasn't even hurting anymore, and she wondered if it had truly been broken or if that had just been a ploy to keep her here. She laughed and cried, letting the water mix with her tears.

She screamed and jumped, slipping on the slick base of the shower, and landed on her ass when the door cracked and crashed open. She looked through the fog-shrouded glass to see three very concerned and pissed-off males. And they were all totally naked. Brock and Mikhail were sporting the biggest erections she'd ever seen in real life, and Jonah's cock was twitching to life again. She pushed herself back into the corner of the shower and watched them with trepidation. They walked toward her with predatory grace, their cocks bobbing up and down and side to side as they moved. They obviously didn't care they were naked.

Michelle eyed Brock warily as he reached for the shower door and swung it open. He stepped inside the large cubicle and crouched down in front of her.

"What's wrong, baby? Why did you run? Why are you crying?" he asked and gently reached out to tilt her face up.

Michelle didn't want him to be nice to her. That only seemed to make the tears fall faster. She didn't know if she could explain the way she felt. She'd been buried so deep for so long, she was confused about what these three men made her feel. And they were werewolves, for God's sake. She'd only ever thought werewolves were fiction. To find out they were real, and that she was mate to three of them, was just too much to comprehend.

"I don't know," Michelle whispered then hiccupped. She laughed at the inelegant sound she made. She hated to cry in public. She wasn't prim and proper when she cried. She was undisciplined and inelegant.

"Talk to me, Michelle. We can't help you if we don't know what's wrong," Brock reiterated.

"He laughed at me." Michelle groaned then covered her face with her hands. She snorted as the plaster on her hands squished under her face.

"Look at me, Michelle," Jonah commanded.

Michelle lifted her eyes in time to see Jonah shove Brock aside, making room for him to step into the shower cubicle as well. Luckily it was so huge. Otherwise they would all be plastered up against one another.

"I wasn't laughing at you, darlin'," Jonah said, reaching out to cup her cheek. "I was laughing because marking you, then claiming you as my mate with my body, had me so filled up with joy, I just...couldn't contain my emotions. You have no idea how long we've waited to meet you, our mate. We had almost given up hope of ever finding you. You've given us a precious gift, darlin'. I will always treasure the memory of taking your virginity."

Michelle swallowed around the tight lump of emotion in her chest. She couldn't believe such an arrogant alpha male was talking to her about his feelings. She'd never expected such profound words from Jonah. She knew she probably looked like a fish out of water when she realized her mouth was gaping open. She closed her mouth with an audible snap as her teeth connected. She could still see the three men were concerned for her emotional well-being and didn't know what to do. She couldn't tell them she was full of joy at having given her body, her virginity to Jonah. So she didn't reply at all, just sat there in the base of the shower and stared.

Brock reached out toward her and took her injured hand between his two hands. The sound of him laughing as the cast made a squelching noise had her smiling up at him.

"How does your arm feel, baby?"

"Good. It doesn't hurt at all anymore. Are you sure it was broken?" Michelle asked uncertainly.

"Yeah, baby. We've claimed you, marked you. Our DNA is mixing with yours, and you will find you'll heal a lot faster than you would have normally. Your sight and hearing will be more acute, as will your sense of smell. You'll feel stronger and will be healthier than you've ever been in your life. Let's get this mess off you. Just be careful you don't overdo it and hurt yourself. You aren't quite healed properly yet and probably won't be until the morning."

Michelle held still as Brock slid the soft goop from her arm. He then picked up the shower gel, squirted some into the palm of his hand, and gently washed the residue from her skin.

"I can wash myself, you know."

"I know you can, baby. Indulge me. I love taking care of you. We all do," Brock replied.

Michelle stood at his urging and let the water stream over her as he washed her, rinsing the suds down the drain. When he was done, he placed the sponge back on the shelf and reached for the shampoo. Michelle moaned under his gentle ministrations as he massaged her scalp and then down the long length of her hair. He pulled her back into the stream and rinsed her hair clean. Then he reached around her and turned the faucets off. He held her elbow as he guided her into the waiting arms of Mikhail.

Mikhail had a large towel ready and wrapped it around her body. He reached for another towel and began to gently rub her hair dry. Once done, he picked her up and set her ass down on the bathroom counter, in between the double sinks. He bent down, rummaged in a cupboard, and stood back up, hair dryer in hand. Michelle had never had anyone play with her hair or head before, and couldn't prevent her moan of delight as Mikhail finger combed her hair and he ran the hot air from the dryer over its length. She'd never felt so pampered or cared for before and wasn't sure what to make of it. Of course, she liked it, but was too afraid to get used to it. For all she knew these three men could change their minds and end up discarding her just like they had Kirsten. Since there was nothing she could do about it now, she closed her eyes and enjoyed the sensations. It wasn't long before the hair dryer was turned off and put away.

"Do you know how gorgeous you are? You are the most beautiful woman I have ever laid eyes on." Mikhail growled against her ear.

"How can you say that? It's not true," Michelle replied.

"Oh, honey. Yes it is. Come here and I'll show you," Mikhail said in a low voice, holding his hands out to her.

Michelle reached toward him and let him lift her down from the counter. He turned her around by placing his hands on her shoulders and met her eyes in the mirror on the wall.

"I'll tell you what I see," Mikhail began.

Michelle watched hesitantly as he reached up between her breasts and pulled the end of the towel from where she had tucked it in. He pulled the towel from her body and stood staring at her image as she stared at his face.

"I see a fiery, passionate woman, petite in stature, but with luscious, full breasts, a tiny waist I could span with my hands, and nice, rounded hips. She has long brown hair with streaks of gold and red fire running through it and full, pouty lips, which make a man want to devour them. She has the lightest, greenest eyes I have ever seen and skin so soft and creamy pale, it's almost translucent.

"She is compassionate and will always stand up for the underdog because she has been the underdog most of her life. She is prim and proper on the surface, almost to the point of being a prude. She covers herself with shapeless clothes to hide her real personality. But underneath all that she is a real firecracker. If she would only let herself go totally, she'd be real wild. Just the way I like my women. She's scared because she's never had anyone to rely on. She's had no one to give her hugs, or take her pain away.

"She is the most beautiful, sexy woman I have ever laid eyes on."

Michelle had tears streaming from her eyes. She had only known these men for such a short amount of time, no more than twenty-four hours, and they already had her pegged. To hear Mikhail talking about her like that, with reverence in his voice, had her heart filling with love. She looked into his silver-gray eyes and saw the sincerity behind his words. Her eyes slid to Brock then to Jonah, and they each had gentle smiles on their faces as they nodded their agreement. She'd never felt so loved and cherished in her life. She had seen the way these men looked at her, but had ignored it. She had hoped to keep her heart locked away from them but that hadn't worked. They had just shattered those barriers to pieces with their lovemaking and words.

She could see the love they had for her shining out at her and knew she wouldn't be able to leave them. Not ever. She had deep feelings for them but still wasn't sure if it was love, and couldn't say the words yet. It was too soon, and she wanted to be sure what she was feeling was love and not just happiness at being loved for the first time in her life for who she was. She turned around and wrapped her arms around Mikhail's waist, giving him a hard squeeze, and she placed her forehead on his chest. The sound of his strong heart nearby was a comforting sound. One she knew she would never tire of.

Michelle gave a protesting squeak as Mikhail picked her up in his arms and strode back to the bedroom. He laid her down in the center of the mattress and followed her down.

Chapter Ten

"You are so special, Michelle."

Mikhail covered his mate's body with his own and kissed away the tears on her cheeks. Then he lifted his head and stared down into her light-green eyes. He could see the growing love she felt for him shining back at him, but knew she wasn't ready for any heartfelt declarations as yet. He lowered his mouth to hers and thrust his tongue in between her full, pouty lips. The taste of her swept through his bloodstream, firing his arousal to flash point, but he knew she wasn't ready yet. He tangled his tongue with hers, mating with her mouth until neither of them could breathe.

He kissed and licked his way down her neck, nibbling on her flesh as he went. He reached her chest and sucked a nipple into his mouth, flicking it with his tongue until it stood up hard, begging for more of his touch. He released that nipple and nuzzled his way over to the other one. He sucked it into his mouth and gave it the same treatment until it, too, was standing up at attention.

He licked and sucked his way down over her flat belly, using his knees to pry her legs apart, and slid his hands beneath her, grabbing handfuls of her ass and kneading the soft globes. He slid down a little further and sucked her clit into his mouth. The sounds she made as he loved her with his mouth only spurred him on to drive her higher into the flames. He released her clit and licked down through her now-slick folds, the scent of her musky arousal taking him to the limit of his control. He fucked her with his tongue, knowing his saliva would help heal any soreness she had left from his brother making love to her. When he felt the walls of her cunt shiver and clench around his elongated tongue he knew she was close to climax.

Mikhail reluctantly withdrew his tongue and moved back up over his mate. He took her mouth with his at the same time he surged into her body, only stopping when he was balls-deep. He held still as her flesh rippled around his hard cock and waited for the pressure to ease. He knew if he began to move too soon, he would reach his release way too early. He weaned his mouth from hers as her grip around his hard shaft lessened and watched her face as he began to move.

He pumped his hips, sliding his cock in and out of her hot, wet cunt, and knew he was in heaven. With every forward thrust he picked up the pace until his balls were slapping at her flesh. He pulled her up with him as he now sat on the bed upright and wasn't disappointed when she wrapped her arms and legs around his body. He clasped her buttocks in his hands and began to knead her flesh, spreading her cheeks, opening her ass, stretching her. He helped her rock against him, and when he felt her begin to ripple around him once more, he pulled her down onto his cock and held her still.

"No. Don't stop. I need you to fuck me," Michelle sobbed out.

"Don't worry, honey. We'll give you what you need. Just hold still for a minute or two," Mikhail rumbled out.

"Why? I need to come, damn it."

"And you will, baby," Brock said. "I just need to prepare you so I don't hurt you."

"What?" Michelle said with a frown, when Brock's wet fingers massaged her ass. "No. You can't touch me there."

"Sh, honey. We'd never do anything to hurt you. Brock needs to claim you, too, and we all know you're already tender from Jonah and now me. If Brock fucks your ass, you won't hurt as much," Mikhail rasped out and held her hips still. He knew when Brock began to massage more cold lube into her ass because he felt her flinch.

"Just relax, baby. No, don't tighten up, it'll only make you more uncomfortable," Brock rumbled. "Yeah, baby. That's it, relax that pretty little ass for me."

"Oh God. You're too big. You'll never fit," Michelle wailed. "You'll rip me in half."

"It's all right, honey. Brock knows what he's doing. Take deep breaths and relax," Mikhail soothed, using a little of his Alpha power to help to get his mate to relax.

"You're doing great, baby," Brock murmured.

Mikhail knew Brock had penetrated Michelle's anus because she had just gotten tighter around his cock. He ground his teeth together and gripped her ass cheeks a little firmer, but was careful not to hurt her. He spread her cheeks wide and knew his brother was pushing his fingers into their mate. The sounds she made and the feel of her flesh clenching around him was way too good. His was in danger of shooting off.

"Michelle, relax, honey. I've got you. Just let go and let us pleasure you." Mikhail groaned out.

"Hold her still, she's gonna go wild." Brock panted.

Mikhail heard his brother squirt lube into the palm of his hand, the moisture making a squelching sound as Brock covered his cock with lube. He felt Michelle flinch then moan as she pushed her forehead into his chest.

"Oh my, it hurts. What are you doing to me?" Michelle asked.

"Shh, honey. Deep breaths, remember. Just concentrate on my voice and relax those muscles. That's it. Good girl. The pain will be gone in a minute and then we are going to make you feel so good," Mikhail whispered against her ear.

"Hurry the fuck up, Brock, or I'm not going to last," Mikhail sent to his brother telepathically.

"Me neither," Michelle replied.

"Honey, did you just hear me talking to Brock?" Mikhail asked, totally astounded.

"Well, duh. I wouldn't have answered if I hadn't," Michelle replied.

"Baby, your ass is so tight, I can hardly stand it," Brock stated in his mind.

"Just shut up and fuck me, damn it. I'm so close," Michelle pleaded.

Mikhail couldn't believe his mate had heard them through their telepathic link, but was not willing to discuss it with her now.

"I'm in," Brock groaned. "She gonna milk the cum from my balls, if she doesn't stop squeezing."

Mikhail had to move. He was too far gone. He was so close to the edge, and he wanted to make sure Michelle reached her peak first. He slid his cock out and then surged back in, taking it slow and easy, letting their mate get used to having two cocks in her body. As he eased in, Brock eased out. They set up a slow, easy rhythm, not pumping into her too hard or fast. The sounds Michelle made as they loved her were a huge turn-on to him, and he knew Brock felt the same. He knew his face no doubt mirrored his brother's as they made love to their woman. He could feel her internal muscles coiling around his cock, squeezing him harder, and knew she was close. He gave Brock a nod over her shoulder, and Mikhail picked up the pace of his thrusting hips. He and his brother pleasured their mate as well as themselves because they were now pounding in and out of her tight holes.

Mikhail felt Michelle jerk in his arms and looked down at her. She threw her head back, her cheeks a rosy-red hue with her passion, her face slack with pleasure, and she cried out as she tipped over the edge. She screamed long and loud, her muscles contracting around his and Brock's cocks as she climaxed. He felt the tingling at the base of his spine and pumped into her harder, faster, and deeper. The feel of her massaging his cock as she climaxed was pure heaven. He roared as he felt his balls draw up close to his body, and then he was spewing load after load into his mate. The sound of his brother's yell reached his ears, and he knew Brock had also found his own release.

Mikhail wrapped his arms around Michelle's waist and held her tight to his body as the last of her climactic tremors faded away. She slumped against his chest, and he breathed in her scent, which was now a combination of her, him, and his brothers. He held her tight and didn't want to let her go, ever.

Mikhail heard Michelle whimper, and he lifted his head to see Brock grimace as he withdrew his cock from her ass. His brother picked up their mate and walked to the bathroom with her in his arms. He glanced over to the side of the room when he saw Jonah move and stand from where he'd been sitting. Mikhail was in awe of the fact Jonah had let him and Brock pleasure Michelle by themselves. Usually his brother was the one directing their love play. But he knew it was different with their mate. They weren't playing. It was for real and hopefully forever. Their mate had already wormed her way into their hearts.

Chapter Eleven

Michelle sat in the backseat of the large truck Jonah drove. Brock was in the front passenger seat, and Mikhail was in the back. They were on their way to her cottage to pick up some clothes for her. She needed them for work tomorrow since her arm was healed and she had won the argument with Jonah about her returning to work. She also needed clothes so she wouldn't have to walk around in borrowed T-shirts. As much as she loved wearing her men's T-shirts with their lingering scent on the material, she knew she couldn't live in their clothes for the rest of her life.

Michelle was surprised she didn't need to direct Jonah to her place.

"How do you know where I live?"

"When I knew you were our mate, I looked up your employee information," Jonah replied and looked at her in the rearview mirror. She could tell he was smiling by the crinkling at the corner of his eyes.

"When did you know I was your mate?"

"The night I found Mikhail bailing you up in the library parking lot," he replied.

Michelle turned to Mikhail. "It was you then and not a pet named after you?"

"Yes, it was me, honey. I knew you were our mate as soon I scented you. I had gone out for a run and ended up in the trees behind the library. I smelled you as soon as you exited the library building."

"You scared the shit out of me. You bastard, I thought you were going to eat me," Michelle said with a laugh and slapped Mikhail on the arm.

"I was going to eat you, honey, and I did, remember?" Mikhail replied and waggled his eyebrows at her.

"You are impossible," Michelle said with a laugh and turned to look out the front windscreen as Jonah pulled the truck to a halt close to her house.

Her three men were out of the truck before she was even unbuckled from her seat belt. Brock stepped back and opened the door for her. She watched as her three men growled low in their throats when they sniffed the air. She felt the fine hairs on the back of her neck rise at the sounds.

"Stay in the car, baby," Brock advised with a growl. "Give me your keys."

Michelle handed her house keys over, then released the breath she didn't know she'd been holding. Brock closed her in the truck, and she watched as her three mates cautiously kept sniffing the air. She saw Brock hand her keys over to Mikhail, and he disappeared around the side of her small house. She watched as Mikhail went to insert the key in the lock, but to her horror the front door swung open. Mikhail and Jonah disappeared inside. She cracked the door to the truck open just in time to hear angry snarls. She didn't stop to think. She bolted from the truck and raced to her front door and into her living room. The sight that met her eyes nearly made her knees buckle beneath her.

Everything was ruined. Her furniture had been slashed, the stuffing pulled out of cushions, and her stereo and television had been smashed to pieces. Nothing had survived. She walked down the small hallway and stood in the doorway of her bedroom. Her clothes were in pieces, her bed ruined. The smell of urine was strong in her room, and she couldn't prevent herself from gagging. Her mates turned toward her, and the angry looks on their faces was her undoing. She began to cry. There was blood all over her walls. The fluid had dripped down the wall, but the words were still legible.

You will die, bitch!

Michelle bolted from the room and ran to her kitchen. The sound of broken crockery crunched beneath her feet. Nothing was left. Her whole life ruined in an instant by some sick bastard. She turned the cold faucet on and splashed water on her face and let the cool, soothing liquid run over her wrists. *Who would do such a thing? I don't even really know anybody, besides my mates and Kirsten. No, she couldn't have done this.*

"Michelle, are you all right, darlin'?" Jonah asked from behind her.

Michelle turned the faucet off and turned to face him. "Who would do such a thing? It took me years to get all the things I had and now they're all ruined."

Michelle stepped forward into Jonah's arms and hugged him tight. She hadn't even realized she was shaking until her body came into contact with his.

"Darlin', I know you're devastated about your things, but I'm just glad you weren't here when they came. You could have been killed. Your things can easily be replaced. You can't. I don't know who did this, but I do know what," Jonah said, and she heard the fury in his voice as he snarled out the last.

Michelle leaned back to see his face and would have cringed if the ire on Jonah's face had been directed toward her. "What do you mean, 'what?'?"

"Wolves," Jonah replied.

Michelle knew her face showed her puzzlement as she frowned up at him, and then light finally dawned. "Werewolves did this? Why? What have I ever done? I didn't even know werewolves existed until recently."

"It's all right, darlin', I'll get to the bottom of this. It has to be rogue wolves, and when I find them I'll rip them apart. This is my territory, and no one is allowed on my land without my permission. Whoever it is will be found," Jonah stated, leaned down, and kissed her on the temple.

Michelle leaned her forehead on his chest and sighed. She knew there was no way she could talk him out of finding the wolves. He was an Alpha, and his job was to protect his own. Even she knew that. This was different from what Kirsten had done, and she didn't feel an ounce of empathy for the rogue wolves. They deserved everything they got.

"Come on, let's get you out of here. I'll take you into town, and you can pick out some clothes," Jonah suggested as he scooped her up into his arms.

Michelle didn't protest at being carried this time. She was still too distraught, and her knees were still shaky. She snuggled into his neck and sighed. Who'd have thought she'd ever be in a relationship with one man, let alone three?

Jonah placed her on the backseat of the car and gave her a peck on the lips. He made sure she was buckled in then closed the door. She watched the sinuous grace of his muscular body as he walked around to the driver's door. He slid in behind the wheel and started the vehicle. Michelle saw Brock and Mikhail exit her house, closing and locking the door behind them. They got into the truck, Jonah shifted the gear stick, and they were off. They drove in silence, and Michelle wondered what was going through her mates' heads. Nothing good, she was sure.

It didn't take long before Jonah was pulling the truck into a parking space, and he turned off the ignition, turning toward her.

"I want you to pick out anything you need, and I don't want any arguments about the cost. We are quite well off and can afford for you to have anything you want and need. Okay?"

"All right," Michelle replied, and then Brock was helping her down from the truck. He clasped her hand in his own and led her to a small boutique-type store. As soon as they walked through the door,

Michelle knew this wasn't an ordinary store. The place screamed wealth, and she knew the clothes would be designer label. She looked up at Brock but didn't get a chance to protest.

"You already agreed, baby. You can't back out now. Go and pick out some clothes and don't look at the price tags," Brock said and gave her a smile.

Once she let herself go and began to choose clothes, she felt like a little kid in a toy store. The quality and the cut of the clothes were superb. She decided since she was now mated, that there was no need for her to choose uptight schoolmarm clothes. She picked a few dresses which she knew would fit like a second skin, short thigh-length skirts, stretchy tops, and lingerie. Lingerie was one thing she'd never skimped on before, and she didn't plan to start now. The young woman behind the counter had come out and helped her choose clothes. By the time she was finished, the sales counter was piled high with outfits, shoes, and lingerie. Her men had even added a few pieces to the pile themselves. She stared in horror at the cash register as the woman rang up the sales. Mikhail must have seen her looking, because he walked up behind her, wrapped his arm around her shoulder, and began to steer her toward the shop door.

"We'll be at the diner. I think an early lunch is in order," Mikhail said and then steered her out the door.

"But..." Michelle began.

"No buts, honey. Let's get some food. I'm hungry."

"You and your brothers are always hungry. I can't believe the amount of food you eat. You should all be fat."

"We're werewolves, honey. We have fast metabolisms," Mikhail said with a grin.

They walked for half a block, and then Mikhail steered her through the door of the diner. He led her to a booth in the back and held her elbow as she sat down and scooted around the long curved seat to make room for him. Besides, Jonah and Brock would be joining them soon, and she loved to feel safe and secure, surrounded by her men. She'd never had that before and intended to relish the experience. Michelle looked at her watch and was surprised to find it was nearly noon. She had no idea so many hours had passed. She looked toward the door of the diner when the bell above gave a tinkle and watched Jonah and Brock stroll toward her. *God, are they hot. I can't believe they are my mates. They make me horny when I just look at them!*

"We're glad you think so, darlin'. I can't wait to get you back home. We are going to fuck you until you're deaf and blind," Jonah replied through their new link.

"I can't believe you heard that. Are none of my thoughts my own?"

"Yes, your thoughts are private, but you shouted that thought in your head. We couldn't help but hear, baby," Brock replied.

"Get out of my head. I don't want you in there all the time," Michelle protested indignantly.

"You're the one in our heads, honey. Don't worry, we'll teach you how to keep your thoughts to yourself," Mikhail said and gave her a sexy wink.

Michelle squirmed in her seat, trying to relieve the ache in her clit and clenching pussy. She felt a gush of fluid leak onto her panties, making them wet.

"I can smell your cream, baby," Brock said as he sat down and slid around to her side. *"Spread your legs for me."*

"What? Oh no way. Keep your hands to yourself," Michelle shrieked and slapped at Brock's hand as it wandered up under her new thigh-length skirt. A waitress came to take their order, and Michelle was relieved when she left, because Brock had taken advantage of her distraction. He slid his hand further up beneath her skirt.

"Will you cut that out?"

"No, baby, I can smell your need. What sort of mate would I be if I left you this way?"

"One who does what his mate asks of him?"

"Spread your legs and let Brock pleasure you, darlin'," Jonah stated through their mental link as he looked at her with determination.

Michelle complied without hesitation, then snapped her legs closed around Brock's hand as he reached the juncture of her thighs.

"You can't do this. Everyone will know what you're doing," Michelle gasped.

"Then you'll just have to keep quiet, won't you, darlin'?" Jonah replied.

"Oh my," Michelle said as Brock's hand slid under the elastic of her panties. She couldn't contain her gasp as the pad of his finger slid up through her folds, gathering her juices, then began to stroke over her clit.

"You like that, don't ya, baby? You like it that we could get caught. That someone could see my hand in your pants. Oh yeah, that's it, squeeze my fingers."

Michelle couldn't believe Brock was fucking her with his fingers. He'd moved from the top of her slit and thrust two fingers deep into her pussy. He moved his thumb to her clit and began to rub the hard little nub as he pumped his fingers in and out of her cunt. She could hear the wet sucking sounds her vagina made as he fucked her and hoped no one else could. She was so close. He had taken her from horny to the precipice in moments. Her eyelids slid closed, and she felt the internal tremors as her walls tried to suck his fingers in deep. She opened her eyes and looked at Brock with desperation. She was about to come and didn't know if she could keep quiet. Brock shifted in his seat, leaned down, and slammed his mouth over hers. He was just in time to muffle her shriek of completion. She felt her body jerk as her pussy gushed her release onto her panties and Brock's hand. The sexy bastard shocked her when he brought his hand to his mouth and licked it clean. He had a shit-eating grin on his face, and his eyes were feral with his desire.

Michelle glanced over to Mikhail at her other side and then to Jonah. They all looked like they were ready to bound to their feet and haul her ass out of there. The waitress returned with their orders and placed them on the table.

"Can I get you anything else?"

"The check, now," Jonah replied. "We'll be taking our food with us."

"No we won't. We're going to sit here and enjoy our meal and not make any extra work for anyone," Michelle stated, folding her arms across her chest beneath her breasts.

Her men groaned but didn't argue. They picked up their burgers and began to eat.

Chapter Twelve

Michelle was out of the truck and inside before Jonah had even turned off the ignition. She ran up the stairs and entered their suite of rooms. She laughed hysterically as she stripped out of her clothes. She could hear her men's feral growls as they ran after her. She slammed into the bathroom and turned on the shower. She washed in two seconds flat, turned off the faucets, and stepped out. Her mates were all crowding around the bathroom door staring at her. She reached for a towel, but Jonah caught her hand in his. With a flick of his wrist he had her wet body smacking into his.

"You won't be needing a towel, darlin'. We'll dry you off…with our tongues." Jonah growled.

Michelle laughed when he picked her up and slung her over his shoulder. She clung to the waistband of his jeans to hold herself steady, but knew she wasn't in danger of falling. Jonah would keep her safe. Jonah righted her and slid her down the length of his body, until her feet landed on the bed. He let go of her hips and gave her a little shove, making her fall back onto the soft mattress. She gave a small laugh then spread her legs wide and slid her hand down over her abdomen and into the top of her slit. She moaned as she touched her sensitive clit and raised her eyes to her mates'. They were all staring at her as she pleasured herself while they removed their clothes. She groaned when she saw Jonah's hands shake and knew he and his brothers were as aroused as she was.

She kept her eyes on Jonah as he stared at her heatedly. When he was naked he crawled up onto the bed and dove for her pussy. She closed her eyelids as he licked her from ass to clit and back again, all the while making small growling noises in his throat. She groaned as he slid two fingers into her cunt and began to pump them in and out of her, hard, fast, and deep. He had her on the verge of climax. He withdrew his fingers, and she felt him slide them down to the puckered flesh of her anus. She opened her eyes, and her gaze connected with his.

"Keep your eyes on me, darlin'."

Michelle squirmed and grimaced with pleasure as Jonah slid first one wet finger into her ass, then another. He slowly pumped his fingers into her until he could go no further. He lowered his head again, but kept his eyes on hers and opened his mouth to flick her clit with his tongue. Her vision dimmed as she reached her peak, her body jerking uncontrollably as he continued to pump into her until the last spasm of pleasure faded away. He gently withdrew his fingers from her ass, picked her up, and impaled her onto his cock. She cried out with pleasure as his hard flesh stretched her open. He placed his hands at her waist and lifted her up and down onto his cock, making them both groan at the pleasurable friction.

Michelle sobbed out her disappointment as he pulled her from his cock. He turned her around on his lap and began to push his cock into her ass as he gently pulled her down. She reached out and clutched Brock's shoulders as he climbed onto the bed in front of her. When Brock leaned down to kiss her, she tilted her chin up and met him halfway.

She moaned into his mouth as he thrust his tongue between her lips and teeth, tangling his tongue with hers. She felt him grab a handful of her hair and tilted her head, giving him better access to her mouth. Michelle met his tongue thrust for thrust, parry for parry, and swirl for swirl until they were both breathless. He withdrew his mouth from hers, placed his hands on her rib cage, and thrust his hard cock into the depths of her pussy. She moaned out loud, the pleasure her two mates were giving her almost too much to bear.

Michelle turned her head when she saw Mikhail move from the corner of her eye and eyed his cock as he held it before her. She leaned slightly to the side and licked around the hard, mushroom-shaped head. The taste of him exploded on her taste buds, and she knew she would never be able to get enough. She opened her mouth wide and sucked the head of his cock into her mouth. She slid up and down over his shaft, swirling her tongue over the sensitive underside as she did. With each slide and glide, she took him into her depths a little farther. She opened her eyes and looked up into Mikhail's eyes and felt the power of her femininity at the look of pleasure on his face. Just to know that she was giving him so much pleasure was a powerful feeling. She saw him reach over her and then felt his hand in her hair.

"Your mouth is heaven, honey. Yeah, that's it, suck me down. Oh fuck, Michelle. You don't know what you're doing to me." Mikhail growled.

Michelle hummed around his cock and concentrated on relaxing her throat muscles. She took him deeper and deeper, until she felt him touch the back of her throat.

"Fuck yeah, honey. That feels so good. Suck me hard."

Michelle found a nice, steady rhythm, but froze when Jonah and Brock began to move. They didn't move in counterpoint to each other. They began to fuck in and out of her pussy and ass at the same time. She moaned around Mikhail's cock and swallowed the pool of saliva in her mouth. She knew Mikhail liked what she did when he let out a yell. So she did it again and again. The grip he had on her hair tightened, and he began to gently rock his hips, sliding his cock in and out of her mouth. Michelle just relaxed and let her mates take over.

She had never felt so full of cock. She didn't know she could ever feel this way. Her body was so overwhelmed with pleasure. It was so good it was almost painful. The sensation of having three cocks fucking her at the same time was beyond compare. She could feel her womb getting heavy with liquid heat, and her pussy began to flutter.

She felt the muscles in her thighs tense, as did the ones in her lower abdomen. The walls of her cunt began to coil, tighter and tighter, and she knew she was about to go over the edge. She sucked hard as Mikhail fucked in and out of her mouth, wanting to take him over with her.

And then she was flying. She went hurtling up and over the edge of the cliff. Her internal muscles snapped and clamped down on the two cocks fucking in and out of her two holes. She yelled around Mikhail's cock as her body shook with the intensity of her release. She felt Mikhail's cock expand in her mouth, and he began to pull out. She dug her fingers into his thigh and clamped her mouth around his flesh. The sound of his roar as he spewed his release into her mouth and down the back of her throat was like music to her ears. She heard Jonah's yell next as he filled her ass with his cum, and Brock followed not far behind. She licked Mikhail clean, slid her mouth from his now semi-erect cock, and slumped down against Brock's chest. She was glad her mates were strong enough to hold her upright because she'd be damned if she could. Her arms and legs felt like cooked spaghetti noodles, and she had not one ounce of energy left.

Michelle mewed as Brock withdrew his cock from her pussy, and then he helped to ease her off Jonah's half-flaccid rod. She wanted to get up and have a bath, but she didn't have the energy to move. She snuggled into Brock as he cradled her in his arms, and she popped an eye open as she felt him move. He was carrying her into the bathroom. She sat slumped against him as he sat down on the rim of the large spa bath and began to fill the tub.

"Are you all right, baby? We weren't too rough with you, were we?" Brock asked.

"No. Good," was all Michelle could manage as a reply.

"Phew, you had me worried there for a minute."

Michelle didn't reply. She was too content and satiated to even think of words.

"I see we were as good as I said we'd be," Brock said with a chuckle.

Michelle didn't open her eyes, just raised her eyebrow in question.

"I said we'd fuck you deaf and blind. Looks like we fucked you mute as well," Brock stated, and she could hear the satisfaction in his voice.

"Yeah," Michelle replied with a smile.

Chapter Thirteen

"I still think I should go to work tomorrow," Michelle said as she glared at Jonah, sitting in his big chair behind the desk in his study. She'd come downstairs looking for her mates and found them all ensconced in the large study in the back of the house on the first floor. She had stood in the open doorway as they discussed who was going to fill in at the library for her. They had said she could before but had changed their minds since going to her house. She'd heard from Angie they had rescinded that decision. She had stormed in, voicing her opinion about the way her mates were trying to take over her life. She wasn't having it.

"Do you honestly think I'm going to let you spend the day alone in the building after what we found at your house?" Jonah growled. "I've already contacted the sheriff, and he agrees with me. You shouldn't be left alone."

"Then send someone with me. I have a job to do and I'm quite proficient at what I do. I'm not letting you or anyone else tell me how to run my life," Michelle retorted.

"No. I'm putting my foot down, Michelle. I'm not letting you place yourself in danger. That's my final word," Jonah said in a quiet, steely voice.

"Oh, screw you," Michelle yelled and stormed from the room, slamming the door behind her.

"How dare he tell me what to do," Michelle muttered as she stomped through the house, oblivious of the curious stares she garnered. "How dare he think he can run my life. I was doing just fine until he and his brothers came along. Who the hell do they think they are?"

Michelle slammed out the back door and stalked into the large landscaped gardens. She was too angry to really take in the beauty surrounding her. She knew that Jonah was right and that was what made her mad the most, plus being told what to do. She hadn't had to answer to anyone for years, and she wasn't about to start doing so now. She breathed in and out a few times and let her anger fade away. She looked around and saw a bench in the shade of a large tree, right next to a fish pond.

Michelle sat down and watched the goldfish swimming lazily through the water. She had been a bit of a bitch. She was going to have to apologize for her behavior. She hated to be the cause of any angst and knew she would be saying sorry before the day was over. She closed her eyes and breathed in deeply. The scent of roses and lavender wafted on the breeze. It was hot already, and she knew they were in for a long, hot summer.

Michelle heard the bushes rustle off to her right, opened her eyes, and stared intently, trying to see what had made the noise. She couldn't see anything, but she felt uneasy. The hair on her nape stood on end, and she felt as if she was being watched. She slowly stood and skirted around the bench, all the time keeping her eyes on the bushes. They weren't moving now, so maybe it had been a small animal. Still she couldn't shake that feeling. She moved fluidly, away from the bench, and then turned to run.

Michelle's breath whooshed from her lungs as she slammed up against a hard, immovable object. She used her hands and pushed back, but a band of steel wrapped around her upper arms and chest, effectively trapping her. A large palm clamped down over her mouth, cutting off the scream forming in her mouth. She looked up into the blackest eyes she'd ever seen. She had no idea who he was and didn't really want to find out. She brought her knee up and aimed for his groin, but he deflected her blow with a well-placed thigh. She struggled and tried to bite him on the hand, but his grip over her mouth was too firm. She felt another big body move in behind her, but couldn't turn around to see. She was trapped. A sweet-smelling cloth was placed in front of her nose, and as she breathed in, she felt her head getting woozy. She was in trouble. She breathed in deeply, trying to fill her oxygen-depleted lungs, and felt herself sliding into unconsciousness.

"Jonah," Michelle screamed through their newly formed telepathic link just before she drifted away.

* * * *

"Michelle," Jonah roared and leapt out from behind his desk. He ran from the study and through the house, following her scent. He slammed out the back door and ran, his nose leading the way. When he got near the fish pond, he smelled a sickly sweet scent and others of his kind, but not from his pack.

He scoured the area with his eyes, all his wolf senses at full alert, and bent down to pick up a small piece of cloth. It was a handkerchief which had been folded over many times to form a small pad. He brought it closer to his nose and inhaled. He coughed as the scent assailed his sensitive nose.

"Blayk, get out here now," Jonah roared through his telepathic link.

Brock and Mikhail were now out in the garden with him, and he watched as they used their senses and searched for signs of their mate.

"I don't know how they got through security, but whoever they were, they're definitely wolves." Mikhail growled.

"Why the fuck has our mate been targeted? Who the hell would want to kidnap her, Jonah?" Brock asked.

"I don't know. Get Jake, Greg, and Devon to check into the security system. I want to know who has taken our mate. When they have the security footage, I want to see it," Jonah barked out.

"They're on it," Brock replied. "They'll let us know when they have the footage."

Jonah had never felt so out of control. He wanted to track and find the bastards who had taken his mate and rip their fucking heads off. But he needed to know what he was up against before he did anything. The last thing he wanted to do was put their mate in even more danger. Plus, since he was most Alpha male of the pack, he had the responsibility of keeping everyone beneath him safe, including his brothers. He looked around to Brock and Mikhail and was just in time to see them shucking their clothes.

"Brock, Mikhail, stop right now," Jonah ordered, his voice low and deep, full of authority. "We can't just track her and put her in more danger. We need to know what we're dealing with first."

Jonah watched his brothers wrestle with their instincts, the same as he just had. Logic won, and he saw when they pulled themselves together.

"Jake has the security tape of the garden ready and waiting. He says he's never seen these guys before." Brock growled.

"Let's go take a look," Jonah replied and took off at a run, his brothers close to his heels.

Jonah pushed through into the security room and positioned himself to watch the tape. His brothers stood on either side of him. The sight of their mate looking around herself as she sat on the bench with fear on her face had all three of them snarling. Jonah breathed deeply, gathered his control, and then held up his hand to stop his brothers from venting their fury. They saw her slam into a large male who trapped her in his arms. The sight of her trying to fight such a big man did Jonah's heart proud. When the other male crept up behind her and placed the cloth at her nose, Jonah couldn't prevent his howl of fury escaping. Their woman slumping in the bastard's arms had his wolf beating against him.

"Do any of you know who they are?" Jonah growled.

"No, Alpha," Greg replied to him and his brothers.

"All right, I want every pack member shown this footage and I want you three to watch them carefully. Whoever they are had to have help from the inside to get on our land. There's no way in hell they could have done it on their own.

"I have a couple of contacts in the law department. Get me a printout of those faces and send them via e-mail as well. Maybe my friends have an idea on who they are."

"Yes, Alpha," Greg replied and got to work.

Jonah and his brothers stalked from the room and headed for the dining room. That was where they did most of their planning and conferring, but until they had an idea what was going on, they were totally blind.

"You don't think Kirsten could be behind this, do you?" Mikhail asked.

Jonah sighed and sat down at the dining room table. Angela brought over a pot of coffee, mugs, sugar, and milk.

"No. I don't think she's that malicious. She was hurt, Mikhail, and she apologized to Michelle," Jonah replied.

"If you don't mind me butting in, Jonah, I have noticed one of the young Omegas acting strange lately," Angela advised. "Even my Cindy thinks so."

"Take a seat, Angie," Jonah invited and waited until she sat down. "Tell me what you know."

"Young Paul Hunt has been acting all uppity in the presence of the other Omegas in his age group. He's been strutting around like he knows things the others don't. Cindy told me she's seen him loitering near the fence at the back garden. And she actually heard him talking one day. She couldn't hear what he said, mind you, but when she questioned him, he told her to mind her own business."

Jonah turned toward Brock and said, "Find him and bring him here.

"No, don't go rushing off, Angie. Sit down and finish your coffee. I'd like you to be here when Brock comes back with Paul. You can tell me what you think."

Jonah sat up straight in his chair when Brock led Paul into the room. The young Omega looked like he was about to pee his pants.

"Take a seat, Paul. Would you like a coffee?" Jonah asked cordially and watched the young man's chest puff out with his own self-importance. Good, he was beginning to relax. He would be much easier to handle now.

"So, how's the studying going?" Jonah asked.

"Good. I'm getting straight A's."

"Good, good. What is it you're studying again?"

"Medicine."

"Yes, that's right, I had forgotten."

"Jonah, the piece of cloth was covered in chloroform," Blayk advised.

"Now that is interesting," Jonah replied back on their secure link. *"Thanks, Blayk."*

"So you would know how chloroform works," Jonah stated as he stared intently at Paul.

"Yes, sir," Paul replied and swallowed loud enough for them all to hear.

"Hm. And you wouldn't happen to know who kidnapped my mate by any chance?" Jonah asked.

"No, sir."

Jonah moved so fast his surroundings were a blur. He had Paul by the throat and dangling in the air before anyone could stop him. He shook the young man as he yelled at him.

"Don't you fucking lie to me! Your life is in my hands, so if I were you, I'd start talking now."

"They said they would kill me if I didn't help them," Paul rasped out.

"Who are they?"

"They're wolves of the Saturn Pack. They've been buying up the surrounding land and decided they wanted yours as well. They have students on their payroll at college and they threatened to kill me if I didn't help them."

Jonah roared his fury and hurled the young wolf across the room. He landed on his ass in the hallway with a resounding crash then Jonah followed him out the door.

"You could have come to me at any time and told me what was going on, but you didn't. We would have protected you. It's our duty as the Alphas of the Friess Pack to protect all our pack members. What aren't you telling me, boy?"

"Nothing, sir."

"You're lying, I can smell it from here. If you don't tell me what I want to know, you die here, now." Jonah snarled.

"They gave me money so I could set up my own practice once I finish studying," Paul whimpered.

"Did you think I wouldn't have set you up with your own practice? How could you be so stupid? They used you to try and take your home out from under you and you accepted money from them. They kidnapped my mate, your Alpha female. Fuck. Get out of my sight before my wolf takes over." Jonah roared and stormed back into the dining room.

"I've heard of this pack before, Jonah. It was a long time ago, but they've always been trouble. They come from the East Coast and have tried time and again to swindle more land out from other packs. They have more money than they know what to do with, but there are no females in their pack and none of them have found any mates, as far as I know. I'll make some phone calls and see if I can find out more," Angela stated.

"Thanks, Angie," Jonah said as she left the room.

"Jonah, if what Angie said is true, about them not having any female members or mates? That means they're probably after our women as well as our land." Mikhail voiced his concern.

"Fuck it," Jonah yelled and stormed from the room. He was in the security room moments later and on the phone to his police friends. He hung up fifteen minutes later, all the information he needed on the piece of paper in his hand.

"All male pack members are to report to the dining room immediately," Jonah broadcast through the common mental link. They were going hunting, and they weren't leaving until he had his mate safely back in his arms.

Chapter Fourteen

Michelle felt as if she had spent the night on a bender. Her head was woozy, and she was so thirsty her tongue was cleaving to the roof of her mouth. She opened her eyes and then slammed them closed again as her head pounded so hard she felt ill. She breathed through the nausea and slowly opened her eyes again. She was in a strange bedroom, but one with money practically dripping from the walls. Everything was exquisite, from the antique four-poster bed, to the gauzy fabric surrounding the bed and the antique Queen Anne dresser and drawers. She had no idea where she was or who had even kidnapped her. She tried to turn over but couldn't. She was tied to the bed. She lifted her head and studied her bindings. They had restrained her wrists in metal handcuffs which were attached to the headboard. Her ankles were wrapped in soft nylon, but she couldn't see where they were tied off.

Michelle knew she wouldn't be able to escape from her current predicament by herself. Maybe if she kept her wits about her, she could talk her kidnappers into releasing her from her restraints. She closed her eyes again when she heard voices outside her door. Hopefully they, whoever they were, wouldn't realize she was awake. She took a deep breath and released it just as the bedroom door opened. She concentrated on keeping her muscles lax and her breathing deep and even. She heard two sets of very light footsteps and knew they were trying to be quiet. She could also hear their hearts beating and their breathing. She knew then that if whoever had her were werewolves, they would know she was awake. She gave up the façade and opened her eyes.

Michelle eyed the unlikely pair and tried not to laugh. One of the men was tall and muscular with dark hair and even darker eyes. The male beside him was short in stature, with blond hair and blue eyes. His face was so handsome he almost looked angelic. He couldn't be any more than an inch or two taller than she was. They looked so ludicrous standing together staring at her she couldn't prevent her mouth from forming a smile. The short blond smiled back at her.

"Who are you and where am I?" Michelle asked, wiping the smile from her face.

"I am Roman Saturn. I am Alpha of the Saturn Pack. You are in my new home about two hours north of Aztec," the blond answered.

Michelle was stunned. She couldn't believe such a small man was the Alpha to a pack of werewolves. She bit her tongue, hard, so she wouldn't laugh in his face.

"This is my twin brother, Nigel. He is second Alpha to our pack."

"Sure he is, and I'm Swiss cheese," Michelle thought to herself. The two men were nothing alike. She knew nonidentical twins could look totally different, but this different?

"Why am I here?"

"We want the land your mates own. We also want the women," Roman replied.

"Why?"

"Because we have no women of our own. There have not been any women born to our pack for generations and we are in danger of becoming extinct. None of our pack members have had the luck of finding their mates, so I have decided we will take women and breed them. It's of no consequence to us if they are our mates or not."

"You can't do that. You can't just decide to take women already mated and rape them. It's wrong. How are you going to feel if you eventually find your mate? She's going to run the other way if she finds out what you've done," Michelle opined. Hopefully talking some sense into the stupid man would make him think about what he was doing.

"I don't want your opinion. I didn't ask for it," Roman declared.

Michelle was stunned. The man obviously had a volatile temper. The veins and tendons in his neck stood out, and his face had gone very red. She was obviously dealing with a nut job. Maybe his big brother was on a more even keel.

"You know my mates are going to come for me. Do you really want to die? What will happen to your pack when there is no one to lead them?" Michelle asked, looking at Nigel.

"The same thing that will happen if we don't find women to breed with," Roman yelled.

Michelle stared at Roman then Nigel. She wondered why he hadn't let his brother speak. She studied Nigel carefully. There was a flash of something in his eyes, but it was gone quickly. He stood staring back at her with no expression in his amber-colored eyes. Her bladder was protesting, and she wondered if they would untie her. Well, there was only one way to find out.

"I need to use the bathroom. Could you please release me?"

Michelle watched Roman as he eyed her warily. He turned to his brother, gave him a nod, and left the room. Nigel stepped up close to the bed and began to work on the bindings around her ankles. She sighed with relief and moved her aching limbs, trying to get a bit more blood flowing in her veins. He moved up the bed, removed the keys to the handcuffs from his pocket, and released her. She couldn't contain the groan of pain as she moved her aching arms. She rolled off the bed and shook her hands down by her sides, thousands of tiny needles piercing her arms and hands as blood began to flow again. Nigel turned away from her and walked to the left side of the room. He opened the door and showed her the bathroom.

"Can I have a shower while I'm in there?" Michelle asked, turning to face Nigel. The less time she spent with them and tied to the bed, the better. Nigel gave Michelle a nod and she stepped into the bathroom. She closed the door behind her and gave a sigh of relief.

She used the facilities, stripped off, and got into the shower. Now was as good a time as any to try and contact her mates.

"Jonah, Mikhail, Brock, are you there?" Michelle asked, concentrating hard on her mates.

"Michelle! Are you well, baby?" Brock sent back.

"Yeah, I'm okay. I've been taken by the Alpha of the Saturn Pack. I think he has a screw loose. He told me we're about two hours north of Aztec. Can you come get me? I think he plans to try and breed with me," Michelle finished on a sob.

"Shh, darlin', try and stay calm. We're already on our way. Keep your wits about you, honey. You never know when the chance to escape will eventuate," Jonah advised.

"Where are you being held captive, honey?" Mikhail asked.

"In a large bedroom, for the moment. I don't know where in the house the bedroom is situated. I haven't been let out. I managed to get them to untie me. I'm in the shower."

"Good girl. You're doing great, darlin'. Did you lock the door behind you?" Jonah asked.

"It doesn't have a lock."

"Okay. I want you to be as quick as you can, get out of the shower, but leave it running. Get dressed and search the bathroom. Find any weapon you can, scissors, a can of deodorant, anything you can use as a weapon. Is there a window in the bathroom?" Brock asked.

"Yeah, but it's too high up."

"Can you climb onto something and look out?" asked Jonah.

"Yeah, hang on a minute. I'm nearly dressed," Michelle replied. *"All right, here goes."*

Michelle climbed onto the seat of the toilet and then onto the cistern, and she prayed it would take her weight and not send her crashing to the floor. She reached up and opened the small window, looked around in case there were pack members outside, then stuck her head out and looked down. *Shit,* she was too high up off the ground. The place had to be at least three stories high. She carefully lowered herself to the toilet seat and down to the floor.

"It's too high. I can't jump that far," Michelle said, her breathing fast as panic began to set in.

"Take deep breaths, honey. Stay calm. Don't worry, we'll be with you soon," Mikhail advised.

"How long before you get here?"

"We're about an hour away, darlin'. Now, did you find a weapon?" Jonah asked.

"Shit, I forgot. Oh, I've found some scissors. They're not very big, but they're better than nothing. Shit."

"What's wrong, baby?" Brock asked.

"Someone's knocking on the door. Hang on," Michelle said.

"Yes?" she called out.

"Get out now and come back to the bedroom," Roman yelled through the door.

"I'll be there in a minute," she replied.

"A minute is all you have then I'm coming in to get you," Roman yelled back.

"He's given me a minute otherwise he's coming in after me," Michelle whimpered.

"It's all right, darlin'. You have a weapon now. If he's alone, stab him with the scissors as hard as you can. Okay?" Jonah asked.

"Yeah, all right. I don't know if I can do this, Jonah."

"Yes you can, darlin'. Just think about what he wants to do with you and instead of being afraid, get angry. Use that anger and you'll be able to do what you have to when necessary," Jonah advised.

"Okay, I love you. I love all of you. Hurry up and get here," Michelle stated.

"We love you, too, darlin," Jonah replied.

Chapter Fifteen

Michelle took a deep breath, concealed the scissors in the waistband of her skirt, and pulled her shirt over the top. She opened the door and stepped out into the bedroom. Roman was sitting on the edge of the bed, waiting for her. There was no sign of Nigel. He stood up as she moved further into the room and began to walk toward her. She tried to give him a wide berth, but he reached out, taking ahold of her shoulders, halting her progress. She tried to shrug him off, but he dug his bony fingers into her shoulders, causing her to cry out with pain.

"Where do you think you're going?" Roman growled and spun her around to face him.

Michelle stared at him and remembered what Jonah had told her. When she saw lust in his eyes as he stared at her, she let herself feel the fury building up inside her. She fanned the flames and thought about what he would do to other women if she hadn't been here. She glared back at him and knew he could see her anger when he threw his head back and laughed. His laughter sounded like a wild hyena, and she used it to build her ire even higher. She removed the scissors from her waistband, and with the flick of her wrist, she opened the blades up. Just as he began to lower his head she stabbed the silver blades into his chest as hard as she could. She'd aimed for his heart and hoped like hell her aim was true. Being a werewolf, he had fast healing abilities, and she didn't want him chasing after her.

Michelle felt his fingers grip her shoulders hard, and then he released her, staggering back like a drunk until he hit the floor with a thud. She stood staring in shock at the blood blooming from his chest around the protruding scissors. She felt bile rise in her throat but swallowed it back down, spun on her heels, and ran. She made it down to the foot of the stairs, not seeing anything beyond the image of the man lying on the floor with scissors sticking out of his chest. She slammed up against a large, hard body and whimpered with fear. Strong, muscular arms wrapped around her waist, preventing her from falling back on her ass. She slowly raised her head and looked up at Nigel. She had failed.

"Thank you. You don't know how long I have been trying to get out from under his command," Nigel said.

"What?"

"Come and sit down before you fall down. You are safe now, I promise," Nigel said quietly and picked her up in his arms as he took her into a large room off to the side of the entryway. He placed her on a sofa and walked over to the bar on the other side of the room. He poured liquid into two glasses, came back, and handed her a glass. He saluted her with the glass and downed the contents.

Michelle cautiously sipped the liquid and knew it was alcohol of some sort. She swallowed, the fiery brew warming her blood. She knocked back the rest in one gulp, the same as Nigel had. Nigel took her glass and returned to the bar, pouring them each another half a drink before he walked back to the sofa. She took the proffered glass and sipped more cautiously. She could already feel the effects of the potent brew.

Michelle began to shake as reaction set in and quickly placed the glass on the coffee table in front of her. She saw Nigel reach up to the back of the sofa and pull the throw rug down. He covered her with the rug and angled his body toward her, sipping his drink.

"My brother has been lead Alpha of Saturn Pack for many years. It took me a long time to figure out he was using his powers to control me and everyone else we had in the pack. It's true we had no females in our pack and none of us had been lucky enough to find our mates, but we didn't realize how unstable my brother was until it was too late. He already had us under his control. He began to kidnap women from our surrounding area, and he would rape them, trying to get them pregnant. What none of us realized, not even me, his brother, was that my brother was deformed. Apparently my mother had a bad fall when she was pregnant with us, and Roman took the brunt of the fall. It was in the fourth month of her pregnancy and we weren't fully formed. Roman was born without any testicles and there was no way he could ever breed, not even with his mate. He went crazy knowing he could never father a child. He blamed our mother for his deformity, and through the years that bitterness festered. Since she was a female, he began to blame all women. He began stealing and raping them. It was like he was trying to punish them for his own inadequacies.

"I think he went insane with that knowledge, and he began to take it out on our pack. Not that I knew at the time. Our parents were killed in a car accident and the inquest found the brakes on their car had been tampered with. Members of our pack began to disappear and were never found or never returned. Even though I am much stronger than Roman was in body, his craziness made him insanely strong of the mind. He was able to control all of us with his power as Alpha and there was nothing I or anybody else could do to circumvent that power. There is no pack left. I am the only one, and I want to thank you for freeing me from my brother's control when you killed him."

"Oh my God, I killed a man," Michelle muttered as her body shook harder. She felt sick to her stomach at what she'd done. Her eyes darted around the room in her panic as she looked for escape.

"Here, drink," Nigel commanded, holding the glass of amber liquid to her lips.

Michelle reached out and tried to hold his hands, but hers were shaking so much she couldn't get the glass to her mouth.

"Let me," Nigel said, brushing her hands aside, holding the glass to her mouth. He didn't stop until Michelle had drained the contents of the glass. She felt all warm and tingly inside, and she knew the alcohol was thwarting her shock.

"He killed everyone in your pack? Including your parents?" Michelle asked and giggled when she heard her words slurring together.

"Yes," Nigel replied solemnly.

"I'm sorry. I'm not laughing at what he did. That's so horrible, words can't describe how atro…atroc…atrocious," Michelle slurred then giggled.

Nigel smiled at her, but she could see his underlying pain and guilt. She felt so sorry for him, but knew he wouldn't want her pity.

"So there is no one?" Michelle asked and saw Nigel shake his head. He tipped his head back and drained the contents of his glass. He rose to his feet and walked back over to the bar. She watched as he poured another shot, then turned to her, raising his glass with his silent question. Michelle shook her head, giggled, and then smiled ruefully. She was already three sheets to the wind. She didn't need another drink.

"My mates are coming," Michelle slurred. "Let me deal with them when they get here. I don't want you hurt."

"I deserve everything I get," Nigel stated with no inflection.

"No, you don't. Your brother was controlling you. You aren't to blame for what he did."

"I should be held accountable, just as he has. He killed our pack for fuck sake," Nigel said with a roar, spun around, and hurled his glass against the wall.

Michelle flinched, pushed the rug aside, and staggered to her feet. She managed to make her way over to Nigel and took his hand in her own.

"Yes he did, and you would have stopped him if you could have. You can't take the blame for what your brother did onto your shoulders. It will eat you up inside. He was insane. There was nothing you could do. Don't let his insanity become your own. The guilt will tear you up and make you just as crazy as he was."

"I have nothing left. There is no one here to care for, to guide and nurture. He destroyed everything."

"And still, it wasn't your doing. You will come and live with us. Join our pack. You won't be an Alpha, but you can be a Beta, second in command. I won't have you torturing yourself and living alone," Michelle stated.

"Your mates will never allow that," Nigel replied.

"You leave my mates to me. I will have my way and there is nothing they can do or say that will stop me," Michelle said in a firm voice.

"You are definitely a worthy mate to your Alphas. You are fair and compassionate," Nigel replied.

"Shit, they're here," she muttered when she heard a car door slam. "Leave them to me and don't get involved," Michelle commanded and turned to face the door.

Chapter Sixteen

Michelle heard the tires squeal on the concrete driveway and doors slam. The sound of the front door slamming open as it hit the opposite wall made her jump. She stood a few feet from the doorway, her feet planted shoulder width apart and her hands on her hips. She was getting her way and was not backing down until her mates agreed.

Brock was the first through the door. He rushed over to her, picked her up, and threw her over his shoulder. He was on his way out the door again before Michelle could open her mouth, but when she did she stopped him in his tracks.

"Put me down right now," Michelle yelled, authority reeking from her body.

She almost laughed when Brock froze, swung her off his shoulder, and let her feet slide to the floor. Jonah and Mikhail barged around her and Brock, growls rumbling out of their chests and hair sprouting out on their forearms.

"Don't you dare touch him," Michelle commanded as she staggered over to her mates. They, too, froze in their tracks, and when they turned to her, she couldn't prevent the smile forming on her face from their incredulous looks. "It wasn't his fault."

"I don't care whose fault it was, everyone here dies," Jonah roared, his words garbled as his beast began to emerge.

"He's the only one left," Michelle slurred as she staggered over to Jonah and placed herself between him and Nigel. "S–Shit, sit down."

Michelle giggled when Jonah looked down at her with a raised eyebrow.

"Are you drunk?"

"Just a little tipsy," she replied and giggled again. "We have a lot to talk about. I need you all to listen to me, and you won't be touching Nigel at all."

"Is that right, honey? You think you can tell us what to do, to let him live after what he did to you?" Mikhail asked.

"He didn't do anything to me. Please, just sit down and listen. If you don't hear me out, I...I...I won't give you any sex for a month," Michelle stated and couldn't help but laugh at the pained expressions on her mates' faces. But it did the trick. Mikhail and Jonah eyed Nigel distastefully one last time then sat down on the large sofa. Brock walked farther into the room, vaulted the back of the sofa, and landed on his ass on the cushion with a soft thud.

"Start talking, baby. If we don't like what you tell us, I'm going to tan your ass," Brock stated with a wicked grin.

Michelle moved around the coffee table, picked up her empty glass, and gestured to Nigel for a refill. She sat down on the edge of the table and eyed her mates.

Michelle related what Nigel had told her about Roman, his past, and his deformity, along with what she did to Roman to free Nigel from his brother's hold.

"Fuck, Michelle, they kidnapped you. He was the one to hold you captive, while his twerp of a brother drugged you with chloroform," Jonah stated.

"Yes, you're right, but Nigel was under the control of his brother. I know you know what I'm talking about. I don't know how you do it or where the power comes from, but when you give a command in that low voice of yours, like you did to Kirsten, I could feel the power rolling off you in waves. You, and your brothers for that matter, could control the whole pack if you wanted to. Since you're lead Alpha you could probably control Mikhail and Brock as well."

"She's right, you know," Brock said quietly.

"Of course I am," Michelle replied and turned toward Nigel as he handed her another glass of amber liquid.

"Don't you think you've had enough, darlin'?" Jonah asked.

"No. I have had a very trying day," Michelle said then tipped the glass back and downed the contents. She shivered as warmth spread throughout her body, the alcohol making her feel as if she were floating. She gave a hiccup, excused herself, and giggled.

"No more for you, baby," Brock said, removing the glass from her hand.

"I want Nigel to come and live with us. He has no pack left and I want him to join ours," Michelle slurred and raised her chin in defiance.

"What? You can't be serious?" Jonah roared.

"Of course, I'm serious. I wouldn't have said it otherwise," Michelle replied indignantly. "No sex for two months."

Michelle giggled at the sound of her mates' groans. She knew then that she had them over a barrel. She was going to threaten to withhold sex every time she tried to get her own way. Not that she could do without for that long, but her mates didn't know that.

"Why don't you take…Nigel and find the kitchen. You need to get some coffee into you, darlin'," Jonah advised.

Michelle sighed. Even she knew coffee would have no adverse effect on the amount of alcohol swimming in her system. Her mates wanted to talk without her and Nigel in the room. She rose to her feet, staggered, gave a giggle as Mikhail reached out and steadied her, then wobbled across the room. She leaned against the wall in the entryway as she waited for Nigel to lead the way to the kitchen. The sound of his voice had her ears perking up.

"I know I don't deserve to be alive after what my brother has done. If you wish it I will bare my throat to you. I don't expect to be let into your home and pack."

Michelle sighed tiredly and jumped when Nigel appeared in front of her. She knew Nigel had just sealed his fate. There was nothing for her mates to talk over, but she followed him down the hallway and into the kitchen off to the left.

She and Nigel were sitting at the dining table sipping coffee when her mates entered. She saw Nigel watching them warily and reached over to pat his hand. She rolled her eyes as her mates' growls filled the room.

"For goodness sake, grab a coffee and sit down. You don't need to keep the bluster up for my benefit," Michelle said then smiled at Nigel and turned back to Jonah. "Where is the rest of the pack?"

"Outside. They were only to enter on our command," Jonah replied.

"Oh, spare me from arrogant, overbearing males," Michelle muttered and stood up.

"Where do you think you're going?" Mikhail asked.

"Outside. They're probably worried about me. I can't believe you left them out there and haven't let them know I'm all right."

"Baby, sit down. They know you're safe, I used our common pack mental link to let them know," Brock advised with a smile.

"Oh, I forgot," Michelle said and sat back down.

The quiet in the room was deafening as her mates eyed Nigel, but she didn't try to break it. She sat back and relaxed for the first time since finding herself in a strange house. Her eyelids felt heavy, and she knew the alcohol she had consumed was certainly affecting her. She blinked a few times to clear her hazy sight, picked up her coffee, and sipped. She was determined to stay awake until her mates had finished with Nigel, and then she planned to take a little nap.

"Can you promise to be loyal to Alphas not of your own pack? To obey direct orders without question? Think long and hard before you answer. You are an Alpha yourself. You will have no power over our pack at all. If we decide to take you in, you will start off as an Omega and will have to prove yourself and work your way up to being a Beta. You will live at our house and abide by my rules. I know you may have trouble obeying my laws, but I will answer to no one, including you. My word is pack law and you will not question my authority," Jonah stated in a hard voice.

"I won't have any trouble not being an Alpha. In fact it will be a relief not to have any responsibility. To have a responsibility and not being able to fulfill it was slowly killing me inside. I have heard you are a fair Alpha, as are your brothers. I will have no problem working my way up through the ranks and earning your trust. If you are offering, I would love to be a part of a pack again and will live in your house under your supervision without any qualms," Nigel replied.

"Then bow to your Alphas and their mate," Jonah demanded.

Michelle watched as Nigel rose to his feet, moved around the table, and knelt with his head bowed to her mates in obeisance. The sight of her mates touching Nigel Saturn on the shoulders in acknowledgment had tears forming in her eyes and running down her cheeks. Her men removed their hands from him, and then Nigel was turning to her. He placed his head on her knee in supplication.

"I am sorry for what my brother did to you, but I am also glad he took you. If he hadn't I would not have the opportunity I am being offered and would still be under his control. For that I thank you from the bottom of my heart, my queen."

Michelle was too touched for words. She looked at her mates through her tears and ran her fingers through Nigel's hair. Her eyelids were so heavy now she could barely keep them open. She removed her hand from Nigel's head and let him rise. She saw the tears in his eyes and knew he was thankful and full of new hope. She blinked, and that was the end of her. She couldn't get her eyes open again and felt herself sliding from her seat. She sighed as Mikhail's scent surrounded her when he scooped her up into his arms. She was back where she belonged, safe and sound in her mate's arms, and she was going home.

Chapter Seventeen

Michelle woke up just as they pulled into the driveway of her home. She was surprised she didn't have a hangover after all the alcohol she'd consumed just hours before. She sat up from the position she had been in, draped all over Brock, and smiled as the house came into sight. It was so beautiful, its white columns gleaming in the late-afternoon sunshine. But the house meant nothing without her mates. She turned in her seat, angling toward Brock, and spied the heat in his eyes as he stared at her. She turned her head to find Jonah looking at her the same way.

Jonah pulled the truck into the carport, and she was out of the truck before he had turned off the ignition. It was so good to be home. She turned at the sound of more vehicles and saw a long stream of vehicles coming up the drive. They really had brought most of the pack with them when they'd come for her. The sight of all the cars showed her she had still not met everyone in the pack. She had a lot to learn if she was going to live up to expectations and be a good mate to the Alphas of the pack. She heard a squeal of delight behind her and spun around just in time to see Kirsten rushing toward her.

She hugged Kirsten back as the tall woman squeezed her tight.

"I'm so glad you're safe. Are you well? Did they hurt you?" Kirsten fired at her.

"No, I'm fine," Michelle replied and gave Kirsten a hug, then released her. "There is someone I would like you to meet. He could really do with a friend right now," Michelle advised, looking for Nigel.

"Who?" asked Kirsten.

"Nigel Saturn," Michelle replied automatically.

"Are you crazy?" Kirsten screeched, then blushed. "Sorry, Michelle, but you must be out of your mind."

"I assure you my mate is quite sane." Jonah growled from behind her.

Michelle turned around and ran a soothing hand down over his chest. "Let me do this, Jonah. It was my idea, so I would like to explain."

"As you wish, mate," Jonah replied.

Michelle turned her back to Jonah and watched as the pack gathered before her. They all bowed their heads when she held up a hand and waited for their talking to cease. She took a deep breath, pushed her shoulders back, placed her hands on her hips, and jutted her chin in the air. She was just daring anyone to question her authority.

"We have a new pack member and I will have him treated with nothing but respect. He is a good man and doesn't deserve the blame or to suffer for the sins of his brother. If I find out he has been treated with anything but respect, you will all answer to me. Is that clear?" Michelle asked in her best cool, haughty schoolmarm voice.

"Yes, our queen," the pack replied as one.

"Well, good then. Nigel, come here," Michelle called.

Michelle spied Nigel's head moving through the crowd from the back of the pack. He was so tall he put Brock to shame. When he was standing before her, his head bowed, she reached out and pulled him to her side.

"Raise your head and be proud of who you are," Michelle whispered from the side of her mouth, forgetting that all of the pack members could hear her. She waited until he had done as she asked and spoke to the pack.

"You may raise your heads. I would like for all of you to meet Nigel Saturn. He is a former Alpha of the Saturn Pack and is now an Omega of our pack. He will be working his way up the ranks of this pack until he is a Beta, and I know it will not be long before he has the trust of each and every one of you as well as your Alphas. Nigel already had my trust. Oh, thanks for coming to help with my rescue. You may go," Michelle stated.

Michelle turned to Kirsten to find her staring at Nigel. She then turned to Nigel and found him staring at Kirsten. She stepped back when she heard the low, rumbling growl coming from Nigel and then looked at Kirsten as her higher-pitched growl answered. She watched with amusement and confusion as they both moved at the same time into each other's arms. The sight of their mouths slamming together and their hands roaming over each other's bodies had her cheeks flaming. She turned to find her three mates standing a few feet behind her, opened her mouth, and closed it again. She was trying to be delicate with her question, but for once her brain failed her.

"What's with them?"

"I believe Kirsten has found her mate," Mikhail replied.

"Really? Oh, that is so fucking awesome," Michelle replied and looked at back at the couple mauling each other over her shoulder. "Get a room."

"What happened to the prim and proper mate we met five days ago?" Mikhail breathed into her ear, causing her to shiver.

"I don't know who you're talking about," Michelle replied with a sassy smile and wink.

"I love our mate whether she is prim and proper or all Alpha Queen. She turns me on just by breathing. But what I don't like is to hear my mate cussing." Jonah growled as he took a step toward her.

Michelle could see the predatory look in all three of her mates' eyes and knew they were about to pounce. Anyone would think they hadn't had sex for a month instead of twenty-four hours. She backed away, but her back and ass connected with a warm, hard male body. She didn't need to look to know it was Brock. She inhaled his unique scent, tilted her head up to him, and smiled.

"Do any of you have any idea how much I love you? If you had told me a week ago I would be telling you that, I would have thought you were crazy. Oh wait, I did think you were crazy. When you told me you were werewolves, I was so shocked I laughed at you. Boy, did you prove me wrong. Thank you for coming to my rescue and for keeping me sane when I was so scared. I couldn't have done it without you."

"Yes, baby, you could. You are much stronger than you think. You found a way out. You didn't need us to rescue you at all," Brock said, and she could hear the pride he had for her in his voice. "I love you, baby."

"I love you with everything I have, honey. My heart, my soul, and my body," Mikhail said, taking one of her hands in his own.

"I love you, too, darlin'. Let's go to bed." Jonah growled, shoving his brothers out of the way, picked her up, and slung her over his shoulder. He moved so fast, Michelle had to close her eyes or she was in danger of being ill.

Chapter Eighteen

Michelle opened her eyes when she heard the slam of the bedroom door. Jonah bent down and eased her off his shoulder, her feet landing on the bed. She stood staring into his eyes as he removed her clothes, shredding them with claws protruding from the tips of his fingers. She didn't flinch or baulk because she knew he, Mikhail, and Brock would never hurt her. She kept her eyes on his as he stepped back from her and began to remove his clothes, his brothers moving to his side to do the same. In moments they were all standing before her naked and proud, their cocks bobbing as they moved in synchronization with their heartbeats. They were magnificent. Testosterone and confidence oozed from their pores, and she felt her body heating with desire. Her breasts swelled, her nipples puckered, and her pussy wept. She watched as they each took their hard shafts in hand and began to pump up and down the length.

Michelle was so turned on by the sight her pussy was now leaking copious amounts of fluid which was covering the inside of her upper thighs. She let herself fall back onto the mattress and landed with a soft whoosh as air released from her lungs. She lifted her head, gave her mates a sassy "come and get me" smile, and spread her legs wide. The growls and snarls coming from her mates only made her laugh as they pushed and shoved at each other. Jonah won the tussle, and he made her shriek as he dove on the bed, landing right between her splayed thighs. There was no preliminary. He dove down and covered her cunt with his mouth.

She moaned with relief as he sucked on her wet folds, making slurping sounds as he sucked up her cream and swallowed her juices.

She felt him slide his tongue up between her labia and swirl his tongue over her clit. He thrust two fingers deep into her pussy and began to pump his fingers in and out of her sheath, rubbing over that sweet spot inside her. He was so skilled with his tongue and fingers, he had her on the brink of climax already. He lifted his head from her slit and looked up over her body until he met her eyes.

"Keep your eyes open, darlin'. I want to see your face when you come," Jonah demanded.

Michelle groaned as he lowered his head once more and sucked her clit into his mouth and thrust his fingers into her depths. She could feel her juices leaking out of her body as they combined with Jonah's saliva. The bed dipped on either side of her, and she knew Brock and Mikhail had joined her. They lifted her shoulders up off the bed and propped her up with a mound of pillows. She closed her eyes when they each leaned over her and drew her nipples into their mouths.

"Open your eyes, baby," Brock's muffled voice growled out around her breast.

Michelle could just see over the top of Brock's and Mikhail's heads and met Jonah's eyes with her own as he sucked and pumped hard. Michelle screamed, her eyesight fading as she toppled over the edge into ecstasy. Jonah sucked and pumped on and in her cunt until the last ripple of her climax faded. She slumped back on the pillows and closed her eyes. Her legs were shaking, and she wasn't sure if she could take any more.

She snapped her eyes open as she felt Jonah and Brock move and watched as they traded places on the bed. She groaned, closed her eyes, and covered her head with her arm.

"Keep your eyes open, baby," Brock demanded.

Michelle opened her eyes and stared at him. "I don't think I can take any more."

"Yes, you can, honey. Brock is going to fuck you with his mouth until you come, and then it's my turn. Once we have all tasted your delectable cream we are all going to fuck you at the same time," Mikhail said with a sexy growl.

"You're going to kill me," Michelle whined.

"Nah, baby, we're going to love you." Brock growled and lowered his head.

Michelle kept her eyes on his and couldn't believe how much of a struggle it was to keep her eyes open. Jonah and Mikhail both leaned over her and sucked and nibbled on her nipples. She moaned as she felt Brock's tongue sliding deep into her pussy and couldn't help her scream of pleasure. The sexy bastard smiled, but pushed his tongue into her really deep.

"How?"

"We're werewolves, darlin', we can change our shape." Jonah answered her question about the length of Brock's tongue.

Michelle moaned as Brock slid his tongue over her G-spot and thrust her hips up, pushing her pussy into his mouth. He slid a hand over her lower belly, and his thumb eased down to the top of her slit. She couldn't believe how turned on she was, since she just experienced one amazing orgasm. She could feel the walls of her pussy beginning to ripple around Brock's tongue and knew she was building up to another spectacular orgasm. He thrust his tongue in and out of her body, making sure to slide over her sweet spot. He flicked his thumb over her clit faster and faster, and all she could do was enjoy the ride. Her womb felt heavy, and she could feel her muscles gathering tighter and tighter. She felt Brock squeeze her clit gently between his thumb and finger, and then she was flying. The spring coiling inside her snapped. She bucked and screamed as her body shook uncontrollably, her limbs jerking spasmodically as her whole body rode the wave of orgasm. She saw stars before her eyes and felt her pussy gush out her liquid release. The sounds of Brock slurping down her juices reached her ears as her body began to calm.

"That was fucking incredible, baby. I could eat your pussy and drink your juices all day long," Brock rasped out as he sat up, wiping her cream from his chin. The sexy bastard put his hand to his mouth and lapped himself clean as he stared into her eyes.

Michelle groaned as Brock and Mikhail traded places. She knew nothing she said was going to sway them from their aim. So she relaxed back onto the pillows to enjoy the pleasure being bestowed on her by her mates.

"Close your eyes and relax, honey," Mikhail said as he rubbed soothing hands up and down her thighs.

Michelle sighed, believing Mikhail to be less demanding. Not that he didn't give her spectacular orgasms, because he did. But he wasn't as aggressive or demanding as his brothers. He was the calm after the storm.

Michelle screamed with pleasure and surprise as Mikhail devoured her. She'd obviously underestimated his need, the need to reconnect and display his dominance over her after her kidnapping. He sucked her clit into his mouth, holding the sensitive little bundle of nerves between his teeth as he flicked it with the tip of his tongue. He shoved what felt like three fingers into her depths and pumped into her fast and hard. Her clit was so sensitive she was glad he only used light touches of his tongue, but he thrust his fingers in and out of her at a furious pace. He withdrew his fingers and slid them down to her anus. She felt him coating her little pucker with her own juices and penetrated her with one of those fingers. She felt him twist his finger around and slid two back into her cunt.

Michelle bucked her hips up trying to get him into her ass and pussy deeper, but he wouldn't be controlled. He went at his own pace, slowly pushing further into her ass and pussy as his tongue still flicked over her clit with light touches. She moaned as she felt him slide in deeper and deeper with every forward thrust of his fingers. Her whole body was on fire, and she didn't think she could take much more. Then she felt him hook his fingers up to the top wall inside her pussy, and he wiggled them on her G-spot. Michelle screamed as climax crashed over her in huge waves and she reached nirvana. Her hearing and eyesight left her as she rode out the waves of bliss.

She came back to herself to find her mates all cuddled up around her, stroking her body and limbs as they eased her down from her climactic high.

"You are so fucking sexy, honey. I love you, Michelle," Mikhail declared.

"Me, too," Michelle managed to pant out, her words slurred.

Her mates laughed, their chests puffing up at her state. She rolled her eyes and let them drift closed again.

* * * *

Michelle's eyes snapped open as Jonah gently bathed her sex with a warm, wet washcloth. She looked like she was about to fall asleep, but that wasn't going to happen just yet. He and his brothers needed to fuck their mate in the worst way. His balls were aching, and his cock was so friggin' hard he hurt. He moved off to the side and gave Brock room to move between her legs. He got onto the bed, turned her face toward him, and took her mouth with his own.

Jonah groaned as he swept his tongue into Michelle's mouth and curled his tongue around hers. He drew it into his mouth and sucked on her flesh. He wanted to crawl inside her and never leave. He weaned his mouth from hers, both of them breathing heavily, and turned to watch as Brock slid his hard cock into her cunt. The sight of his brother's cock sliding in and out of their mate's pussy was such a turn-on, he didn't know if he would last the distance.

Jonah helped lift Michelle up onto Brock's lap and watched as his brother devoured her mouth just as he had done. He noticed Mikhail move and turned to see him crawling up behind Michelle, a tube of lube in hand. The sound of Mikhail popping open the top of the lube bottle had Michelle pulling back from Brock and turning her head to look over her shoulder. Jonah took the opportunity presented by her mouth turning in his direction and rose up onto his knees. He held the base of his cock in his hand and thrust his hips forward until the head of his cock touched her lips.

Jonah groaned as Michelle swirled her tongue around his cock then over the small slit in the top. He wanted to shove his cock down her throat, but kept himself on a tight rein, not wanting to push her too far or to hurt her in any way. He saw her open her mouth wide, and then she was sucking his cock into her mouth. The sight of her with his cock in her mouth, his brother's in her cunt, and his other brother working his cock into her ass was his undoing. He grabbed a handful of her hair and began to slide his cock in and out of her sweet, warm, wet mouth. He started off slow and easy, giving his brothers a chance to set up a rhythm as they began to thrust in and out of her pussy and ass. She looked so sexy, all her holes filled to capacity with their erections.

When his brothers were in a nice rhythm and began to pick up the pace, Jonah did as well, keeping up as they all fucked their mate at the same time. Jonah dropped his head down and watched his cock disappear and reappear as he slid it in and out of Michelle's mouth. When he reached to the back of her throat he growled long and low. He pulled back after a moment and glided into her depths again. She must have been ready for him this time because she had loosened the muscles in her throat, and he slid down even further. He couldn't contain his yell of pleasure as his pubic hair touched her nose. She had taken every inch of his cock into her mouth and throat.

Jonah felt her moan around his hard shaft, the vibrations travelling up his length, and he lost it. He pumped in and out of her mouth as his brothers slammed in and out of her body. She sucked on him hard every time he withdrew, then hollowed her cheeks and used her tongue on the large vein on his cock as he slid back in. He felt the warm tingling at the base of his spine and knew he was getting close to his peak.

"She's killing me. Push her over," Jonah commanded his brothers.

Jonah saw Brock slide his hand down between him and Michelle's body and knew by her moan, his brother was massaging her clit. The sound of flesh slapping flesh and rapacious moans filled the air. Jonah felt his balls touch Michelle's chin, and the tingling warmth spread around to his testicles, drawing them up tight against his body. He pumped into her mouth four more times, gripping her hair in his fist, and yelled his release. The sound of her screaming and swallowing his fluids down at the same time told him she had reached orgasm as well. Brock and Mikhail yelled a second later, and they all climaxed together.

Jonah withdrew his wet cock from Michelle's mouth and slumped down on the bed. He had never felt so weak. A newborn kitten could have knocked him over just by breathing.

"She passed out," Brock said, garnering his attention.

"Well, I guess we fucked her deaf, blind, and mute again," Jonah replied with amusement. "I'll go and fill the tub in a minute."

"Yeah, I'll help you, when I can walk," Mikhail said and flopped on the bed, too.

"You're both a couple of pansies," Brock said and staggered to his feet.

Jonah burst out laughing as he watched Brock carry an unconscious Michelle into the bathroom. He could see his brother's legs shaking as he carried their mate and knew Mikhail had seen it, too, as his laughter joined Jonah's.

What more could Alphas of a pack wish for? They had everything they wanted, right there in the bathroom with their brother.

THE END

WWW.BECCAVAN-EROTICROMANCE.COM

ABOUT THE AUTHOR

My name is Becca Van. I live in Australia with my wonderful hubby of many years, as well as my children, a pigeon pair (a girl and a boy). I have always wanted to write and last year decided to do just that.

I didn't want to stay in the mainstream of a boring nine-to-five job, so I quit, fulfilling my passion for writing. I decided to utilize my time with something I knew I would enjoy and had always wanted to do. I submitted my first manuscript to Siren-BookStrand a couple of months ago, and much to my excited delight, I got a reply saying they would love to publish my story. I literally jump out of bed with excitement each day and can't wait for my laptop to power up so I can get to work.

Also by Becca Van

Ménage Everlasting: Pack Law 2: *Keira's Wolf Saviors*
Ménage Everlasting: Pack Law 3: *Mate for Three*
Ménage Everlasting: Terra-form 1: *Alpha Panthers*
Ménage Everlasting: Terra-form 2: *Taming Olivia*
Ménage Everlasting: Terra-form 3: *Keeley's Opposition*

For all other titles, please visit
www.bookstrand.com/becca-van

Siren Publishing, Inc.
www.SirenPublishing.com

Lightning Source UK Ltd.
Milton Keynes UK
UKOW032248010713

213091UK00016B/1153/P